Jonny

The Fog

By

Dave Hopwood

© 2014 Dave Hopwood.

Cover designed by Tim Wakeling.

All rights reserved.

To

Paul Hobbs

Thanks for inspiring me to think bigger

And to

Tim Wakeling

Thanks for your patience, hard work and encouragement

Part One: Through the Roof

Chapter One

One night Jonny Retro had a dream. As he lay on his back staring at the little blue and green patterns on the ceiling, made by the rotating Star Wars lamp beside his bed, a strange thing happened. He began to fall asleep, but not in the usual dreamy, dozy, slowing down kind of way, where his eyelids got heavy and he dropped whatever he was reading and just rolled over and tugged the sheets round himself. (Duvets always made him sneeze.) Instead it felt as if he was still awake, more awake than ever, as if he wasn't asleep at all, and it was as if a door opened in the ceiling and he could step through the gap onto an invisible ladder and climb right through the ceiling and walk into a whole new world.

It was dark, very dark. At first he just thought the bulb had blown on his Star Wars bed lamp. But this was a different kind of darkness. Not frightening in any way. It was an unusual, warm kind of darkness, the kind of darkness where it felt like Jonny's friends had planned a party for him and were just waiting to jump out from behind the sofa with a massive pile of presents and a big cake. Jonny walked around in this darkness for a while. He had never liked the dark, he usually imagined all kinds of monsters waiting there to attack him. But for some reason he just knew there were no dangerous monsters hiding here. He waved his arm in the air and a very strange thing happened. It was as if he could cut a slice in the darkness, because a little line of light shone through where he'd waved his arm. He swirled his hand in a circle and cut a whole ring of light in the air in front of him. The darkness was like a big, warm pie and he could cut big chunks out of it.

So that's what he did. He walked around slicing squares and triangles and circles, and then he started picking them up and rearranging them like a huge jigsaw. Lots of portholes and windows of light started appearing, and not all the same colour. Instead every kind of colour and shade. Blues, greens, yellows, reds, oranges, maroons, pinks, purples, mauves and other colours he'd never imagined before.

Some of the colours looked strange and made Jonny laugh. And that gave him a shock, because his laughter sounded really loud, as if he was shouting in a massive valley. The sound made everything rattle and shake and bits of the darkness began to crumble and fall onto the floor, like crumbs off a giant biscuit.

He yelled as he jumped out of the way to dodge the avalanche of huge crumbs, and as he yelled the noise made more blobs of darkness come crashing down. So he shouted again, and again, and again, and with every shout another blob fell off. Longer words made big slabs of light appear as a big slab of dark popped out, shorter words made little chunks of light appear. He experimented with lots of the words he knew, shouting them all with a huge grin sketched across his face.

'Pterodactyl! Discombobulate! Gongoozler! Braggadocio! Scalextric!'

After a lot of shouting and crashing Jonny found himself completely surrounded by coloured light.

It was obviously a very different world to the one he was used to. He lived at 72 Dagenham Drive, in a house that was small and in a row of houses which all looked the same. The paint was peeling off the doors and windows, and the road outside was always full of parked cars. Dogs were always barking, kids tussled in the street and you could usually hear the wail of ambulance sirens mixing with the chimes of ice cream vans. And sometimes it got confusing and you couldn't tell whether it was time for a Magnum or a broken leg. But this world was not like that.

Colour and light pulsated everywhere, swirling around like a multi-coloured fog, and this fog wasn't wet and cold and clammy like an early morning in February, this was a warm, glowing kind of fog, buzzing with life and colour. Swirly clouds of it kept coming up to Jonny as if they were waiting for him to do something with it.

They even formed a queue.

'They look like people in the queue in the supermarket,' Jonny thought. 'It would be weird if fog could talk.'

'What would we say?' said a voice.

Jonny leapt back and looked all around. The voice was rich and deep, like the sound of a tuba blowing a low note.

'Hello?' said Jonny.

'Hello.'
'Hello.'
'Hello.'
'Hello.'

Other voices started to say hello and the bits of fog in the queue began to wave at him. Some of the voices were loud and deep like a brass band, some were soft and gentle like the sound of his mum sighing after a hard day. Others were squeaky like a mouse scuttling along the skirting board or creaky like an old door opening. 'You can speak!' said Jonny to the line of foggy shapes.

'Well you said we could!' they replied.

'What else d'you want us to do?' said one of the squeaky voices.

Jonny had to think.

'I'd like you to… sit down,' he said.

Crash! Flump! A hundred foggy shadows fell to the ground like a huge pile of coats being thrown onto the floor.

'Get up!' he said and they all jumped up again.

'Sit down!' said Jonny. 'Get up! Down! Up! Down! Up! Down! Up!'

Jonny was starting to enjoy himself.

The foggy shadows shot up and down like yoyos as he called out the orders. Then one of them, a soft sighing one, said,

'D'you mind I think I'm going to be sick - all this getting up and down…'

'Can fog be sick?' said Jonny.

'If you want it to,' said the fog.

Jonny gave a cheeky grin. 'Go on then,' he said.

And the place was filled with one huge 'Bluh!' and lots of multi-coloured sick went zooming round the place. Fortunately foggy sick was not like Jonny's sick, it didn't smell for one thing and it looked fantastic, like a huge river of gold, silver and scarlet tinsel, swirling round his legs and creeping into his socks. He laughed and shook his feet.

Chapter Two

'Stop! No more being sick!' Jonny said.

The gold and silver and scarlet tinsel piled up into a huge, single, shining statue. It stood up straight like a massive, glimmering action man. About two metres tall. Jonny went up to it and said, 'Wow! You look cool.' 'Thank you,' said the statue and the voice sounded like jangling music, like someone strumming an electric guitar.

Jonny held up his hand.

'High five!' he said.

The statue raised a silver hand and slapped it against Jonny's.

'Who are you?' said Jonny, his eyes wide.

'You tell me,' said the figure.

'Er… I know, I'm going to call you Mr Fog. No. Fog Legs. No… I know, the Fog Prince, 'cause you're made of fog and you look like a sort of prince wearing gold armour.'

The Fog Prince nodded. He seemed happy with that.

'What shall we do now?' the prince asked, and some of the other foggy figures came up to see what Jonny was going to say.

Jonny looked around. Everything went quiet and still. No one moved. Jonny had a think. He turned around on

the spot and thought about what to do next.

'Hurry up,' squeaked one of the voices.

'If you can really do anything…' Jonny said.

'We can!' they all said.

'Then let's make a really exciting place. I've always wanted a big adventure park in my garden, with lots of sunshine, and lots of tropical plants and massive trees to climb, and dolphins you can swim with and wild animals you can ride on, and dinosaurs you can chase, and bugs you can catch, and creepers you can swing on, and two summers a year, one long and one short…'

Before he could finish the whole place started buzzing with things happening. The foggy shadows zoomed here and there, round his head and between his legs like dragonflies on an important mission, and as they moved things began to appear from nowhere.

The sky over Jonny's head turned bright blue, and he found himself standing on a cliff edge, and water began to appear below him, splashing against the rocks. The Fog Prince looked up and snapped his fingers and a tiny speck of dust appeared in the blue sky. The speck got bigger and bigger as it fell towards them. It was no longer a speck but now looked as big as a rock.

'Look out!' yelled the prince and he and Jonny leapt backwards out of the way as a huge seed fell out of the sky and landed with a loud 'Plop!' on the cliff top right in front them. The ground began to rumble and little cracks started to appear which then turned into big cracks and with a sudden flump sound the top of a tree punched its way through the surface of the ground and started shooting up and up into the air. It was like a giant worm wriggling its way out of the earth. Suddenly seeds started falling all over the place, the Fog Prince and Jonny were leaping and diving around, trying to dodge them as they crashed into the ground in great clouds of dust. The seeds disappeared for a second, then came snaking up out of the earth as huge trees.

'Let's climb one!' said the Fog Prince, so he and Jonny raced each other up two huge palm trees, that stood side by side.

'First one to get a coconut is the winner!' called the prince.

Jonny climbed higher and higher, his knees scuffing against the rough bark on the tree. He could see the Fog Prince out of the corner of his eye, he was a very fast climber. Jonny often climbed the tree in his grandparents' back garden, but it was nowhere near as big as this one.

'Got one!' called the prince and he grinned at Jonny from the top of his tree waving a coconut.

'Oh! I wanted to win!' said Jonny.

'Maybe next time,' said the prince and he spun his coconut on his finger as if it was a basketball. Jonny plucked a coconut from his own tree and lobbed it at the prince's, it knocked it off his finger and sent the coconut spinning to the ground.

'Hey!' said the prince, 'that's not fair.'

'Never mind - hey while we're up so high – let's make a big doughnut of a sun!'

He looked up into the blue sky, jabbed his finger into it and drew a huge circle. He shouted out 'Yellow!' and

began to paint it a bright yellow with his hands, then he thought,

'I wonder what a blue sun would look like?' so he yelled out, 'Blue!' and started smearing blue all over it. But that was no good – the sun just disappeared in the blue sky. He called out 'Black!' but then couldn't see a thing, everything just went dark. He tried lots of colours and in the end he came back to yellow. Bright, gleaming yellow. Like a huge dollop of honey.

The prince reached into the pocket of his golden tunic and pulled out a beautiful shell. He threw it to Jonny.

'Here – polish this – it'll make a great moon for the night time.'

Jonny breathed on it and rubbed it on his sleeve. The shell changed colour, turned silver and glinted in the yellow sun. Jonny began to blow on it and the shell grew bigger and bigger, like a football being inflated. When it was too big for him to hold he let it go and the shell floated up like a giant balloon and off into the sky.

Chapter Three

'Come on,' said Jonny, 'Let's make some... fish! A big purple and yellow sabre-toothed shark!'

The prince frowned. 'If you say so,' he said, 'race you to the ground!'

And the moment he said this he let go of the tree and went shinning back down again, like a fireman down a pole, faster than a Formula 1 racing car.

'Birds,' said Jonny, 'we must have birds too! Hey you lot! You fog people over there!'

He waved at the waiting wisps of fog, all hanging around looking bored like a bunch of teenagers at a bus stop.

'Come help!' he said.

The Fog Prince snapped his fingers and suddenly the place was ablaze with colour. There was a sound like popcorn popping in a microwave and fish and birds appeared out of thin air, flapping their fins and their wings. Jonny started catching the fish and throwing them into the sea. They were all kinds of shapes and sizes and colours. And some could even talk.

'Where's the sea?' one of the fish said.

'Last one in the water's a fish finger!' said another.

'Out of my way you little smelly plankton - I'm a shark!' said a shark, and it dived over the cliff into the sea below.

The fish jostled and bumped each other as they slipped over the cliff into the sea like a thick slippery carpet.

'Smells a bit fishy,' said Jonny.

'Well, it would do,' said the prince. 'They're fish. Watch out! A golden eagle.'

'Where?' said Jonny.

'Here,' said the prince.

He opened his arms wide and two huge golden wings burst from his foggy chest, then a head popped out and two beady eyes looked around. With a cry the bird shot out, swooped over Jonny's head and flew off into the distance.

'More!' called Jonny.

Other birds appeared from the prince's chest, they swooped out and followed the golden eagle. Sparrows, seagulls, robins, vultures, even a dodo came waddling out and immediately fell and splattered on the floor. The dodo flapped its wings but was getting nowhere. In the end it shuffled away looking for other dodos.

'What now?' said the prince. 'Fish or birds?'

'Both!' said Jonny, 'flying fish!'

And a swarm of flapping scaly creatures flew out from behind a rock and dived over the cliff and into the sea.

Jonny and the prince clapped their hands and whooped and shouted and kicked up the dust and with every move a new bird or fish appeared from nowhere. Tiny specks of dust swelled in the breeze, then wings and eggs popped out with that same old popcorn sound and before you knew it there was a new kind of bird. The same with the fish. Jonny and the Fog Prince would shake their heads and a hundred beads of coloured sweat would flick out into the air and hover there for a while, then Jonny would laugh or sneeze or cough and every single bead of sweat would swell and pop and grow into a different coloured fish with a crooked smile and huge beady eyes. Tiny goldfish and guppies and huge tiger sharks and whales – they all appeared from nowhere and went slithering and sliding over the cliff into the sea.

Jonny ran over to the cliff edge and stood looking down into the glistening blue water below.

'I wonder if I can dive into the sea from here?' he thought. 'It's a long way, but I might be able to…'

He felt like he could do anything in this new world, and just thinking something seemed to make it happen. So before he knew it he had dived upwards into the air, turned a triple somersault in the sky and was heading with his arms stretched forward like Superman right into the deep blue water below. Splash! The water was warm and bright, and he found himself swimming down and down, deeper into the ocean, until he could see plants and fish and little strange creatures down on the seabed, swaying and swimming and scuttling about down there.

There was a flash of gold near him and he glanced over to see the prince swimming under the surface beside him.

'Bluh bluh bluh,' Jonny said. 'Blet's bluh bluh bluh.'

He spoke underwater and though his voice sounded strange the prince could understand and followed him. They swam around for a while chasing fish and exploring the weird sea monsters down there. The creatures were extraordinary colours and had faces like sponges that someone had squeezed and scrunched and dipped in superglue so that strange expressions stuck on them. Double decapusses with twenty huge tentacles came swirling by, and huge tyrannosaurus sharks with teeth like big white axe heads. They didn't attack though, they seemed quite happy living together down there.

The Fog Prince held up an electric blue sponge.

'We could play hacky sack with it!' he said.

'Gloob bluh-bluh!' said Jonny, though why the prince could speak clearly and he couldn't is anybody's guess.

Jonny had never played hacky sack in his life before and most people never played it under water with a bright blue sponge, but he found he was really good at it. They kept it going without missing a kick for quite a while and every time they booted the sponge up in an arc to one another it made a weird noise, a bit like the sound of a cow laughing.

Chapter Four

After a while they swam up to the surface and lay on their backs in the water. Tropical fish swam in between their legs and sharks with huge fins glided around them. A massive vulture swooped down from the sky and sat on Jonny's stomach, singing to itself in a gravelly voice. There was an almighty splash by Jonny's head and he turned to see a huge sea lion splashing about next to him, its whiskers looking like a soggy mop of grey spaghetti round its mouth.

The sea lion opened its mouth and roared so loudly that the sound sent huge waves through the water, so big that a gang of piranhas went past surfing on them.

'I didn't know fish could surf,' Jonny said.

'They can round here,' said the Fog Prince. 'Anything can happen round here.'

And just to prove it he sat up in the water, stood up and started walking on the waves.

'See?' he said, 'have a go.'

Jonny wobbled a bit as he stood up, and the water beneath his toes felt strange, not like solid ground at all, it kept changing shape for one thing. But he steadied himself and had a go and before you could say 'surfing piranhas' he and the Fog Prince were having a race across the sea. They ran for what seemed like hours, and as they ran Jonny watched the land near them change. Jungles, hills, beaches, cliffs, rocks, rainforests – everything went zooming by as he and the Fog Prince raced to keep up with each other.

'Yaha!' Jonny yelled, throwing his head back, and that was when he noticed the crowd racing to keep up with them - seagulls, eagles, falcons, bats, chickens, ducks, pigeons.

He and the prince and the bunch of birds ran for a good long while. Eventually they staggered off the sea and flopped onto a nearby beach covered in golden yellow sand. And there they fell asleep.

When Jonny woke he got the biggest surprise in the world. A giant catfish, with whiskers like barbed wire, was walking up the beach towards him. Jonny began to back away, but the catfish was moving very fast. As it came closer it began to open its mouth, and then it began to suck. And Jonny found himself been pulled along the sand, into the catfish's mouth. It was as big as a cave and he tumbled inside. There was a man in there sitting at a table, wearing a yellow bowler hat, drinking tea and eating a plate of doughnuts.

'Want one?' he asked.

Jonny took one and bit into it. It tasted like chocolate, honey, peanut butter and raspberry jam mixed together, but in a good way.

'D'you live here?' Jonny asked the man.

The man shook his head. 'No, I'm just getting a lift. I'm on my way to a place called Ninevah,' he said. 'I normally go by whale but this catfish turned up first today.'

Just then a tall thin man went past with a plank on his shoulder.

'What are you doing with that?' Jonny asked him.

The man turned to Jonny and clouted the guy sitting down with the other end of his plank.

'Me?' he said. 'I'm building a boat of course. Right next to his tower.'

He pointed to another man passing by with a pile of bricks balanced on his head. The man waved and went off whistling, dust drifting down onto his head off the tall pile of bricks.

'A boat? A tower? Inside a catfish? What's going on?'

'Sometimes you have to do the strangest things in the strangest places,' said the man with the plank, and he turned and followed the man with the bricks.

Suddenly there was an ear-splitting rumbling sound and everything began to shake.

'Look out,' said the man at the table, 'he's going to be sick, we must be arriving.'

And he grabbed three doughnuts and wedged them all in his mouth.

There was the sound of a huge burp and a massive explosion... and Jonny woke up. The catfish had been a dream, he was still on the golden beach next to the Fog Prince. No sign of the man with the plank, or the man with bricks, or the man with the doughnuts.

'I think it's time for the creatures,' the prince said.

Jonny sat up and scratched his head. He had half expected to wake up in his own bed back home, but no, he was still in this strange dreamland where anything could happen. So he nodded and shouted, 'Time for the creatures,' not really sure what that might mean.

The sand on the beach began to vibrate and grow up unto a little hill in front of them. There was a rumbling sound which grew louder and louder and then suddenly the beach exploded and grains of sand flew up into the air and swirled all over the beach. The Fog Prince stood up, put his hands on his hips and nodded.

'You've started something now,' he said.

'Have I?' said Jonny.

'Oh yes!' said the prince, 'just you watch!'

And suddenly the air was filled with the sound of humming, and thousands of grains of sand hovered like a huge swarm of bees. The sound was warm and happy, like a good pop song, but nothing moved, those grains were all waiting.

'What now?' asked Jonny, but he knew really. It was up to him. The sand was waiting to change into animals: cats, dogs, elephants, kangaroos... a million creatures waiting to be born.

Jonny clapped his hands, snapped his fingers and shouted, 'Go!'

And those creatures certainly did.

The grains of sand began to bounce off each other like balls on a snooker table and every time they bumped against each other they grew a new leg or a new head. And then they began to expand like tyres on a car being blown up. Or maybe tyres on a lorry, or a tractor, because they just got bigger and bigger and bigger. One of them got so big it exploded and turned it into a million fluttering buttersquitos. A kind of cross between butterflies and mosquitos.

'What would you really like to make?' the Fog Prince asked.

'If I could do anything?' asked Jonny.

'If you could do anything,' said the prince.

Jonny knew the answer to that one.

'Dinosaurs, dragons and unicorns!' he said.

There was the sound of a roar and a huge flame that licked at Jonny's nose and singed his eyebrows, and for a moment he could hear and see nothing. Then, as he rubbed his eyes and squinted slowly, he saw a huge purple cloud, and when it cleared a large green monster appeared in front of him. It had massive wings, giant claws on its feet and a crinkled mouth that spewed smoke, like a crumbling chimney. It was the biggest creature he'd ever seen. Jonny backed away but the Fog Prince laughed.

'Don't worry!' he said. 'He's your friend.'

The dragon took a step forward and the ground shook like a piece of jelly. It threw its head back and roared at the sky, yellow flames shot out of its mouth, but when it looked back at Jonny it had a big grin on its face.

'Good trick eh?' said the dragon, in a voice that sounded high and squeaky, like it had been speeded up.

'That voice is no good for a dragon like you. What's your name?'

'Cutesy,' said the dragon.

'Cutesy! You can't be a dragon called Cutesy – dragon's aren't called Cutesy. Firebreath Slimetongue, that's who you can be.'

Firebreath Slimetongue shrugged and sniffed and roared at a nearby gooseberry bush. Flames spurted out of his mouth and toasted the bush, but it didn't burn up. When the flames had gone the bush was as green as ever and still full of bright, juicy berries.

The Fog Prince grabbed a handful of the berries and offered them to Jonny. Jonny took them and munched them down, they were sweet and tasted perfect. He'd never tasted any fruit as good as this.

'Have some,' he said, his mouth still crammed with them.

But the Fog Prince shook his head. 'I don't need to eat,' he said, 'I'm not like you.'

Before Jonny could ask why he heard the sound of thundering feet. The Fog Prince dived out of the way as a gleaming white unicorn went charging past. It stopped and turned to look back at Jonny. It lowered its head as if bowing, and it had a single silver horn on its forehead. Jonny beckoned towards the unicorn and it walked over to him. Jonny ran his hand over its velvet nose, then he carefully reached out and tapped the horn with his finger. It sparkled in the sun, like a silver ice cream cone studded with diamonds.

'Wow!' said Jonny. 'That's amazing!'

As he tapped the horn it changed colour and became bronze then gold then went back to silver.

'Shimmersteel. That's what you're gonna be called,' said Jonny.

A deafening snarl made Jonny jump backwards. A shy Tyrannosaurus Rex peeped out from behind the dragon. It had a gigantic head, like a colossal grey rock, and a tail like a thick stone scarf. When it stood up at its full height it was taller than a house.

'Rocktail!' yelled Jonny. 'I'm gonna call you Rocktail.'

He reached out and the T Rex lowered his head so Jonny could pat it. The skin on his nose felt scaly and full of bumps. Rocktail grinned and he showed a line of teeth that were as big as skateboards.

'Climb on his back,' said the Fog Prince.

'How?' asked Jonny.

Rocktail flicked his massive backside round and lowered his tail in front of Jonny.

Jonny grabbed it and scrambled up, as if he was clambering up the side of a mountain. As soon as he was on top the Fog Prince appeared beside him, leant close and whispered, 'Hang on.'

Before Jonny could ask why Rocktail reared up on his back legs and shot off, running so fast that Jonny had to hang on for dear life. It felt great though, Jonny laughed and shouted and screamed as they thundered around jumping over small trees and booting rocks out of the way. They ran and ran until another cliff edge loomed in sight.

'Stop!' yelled the Fog Prince, but Rocktail didn't.

'Stop!' Jonny yelled.

But the T Rex ran on.

'He's going over the

cliiiiiiiiiiiiiiiiiiiiiiiiiiiiiiiiiiiiiiiiiiiiiiiiifffff…'

But he wasn't. Instead Rocktail came screeching to a sudden halt, his toes digging into the ground, making great ragged tracks and huge clouds of dust. However, Jonny couldn't hold on any more and he shot forward and went flying over the dinosaur's head. They had come to the edge of the cliff by now and Jonny flew over the edge and started falling down the massive drop. He fell for a long time, the wind ripping at his clothes and making his hair stand on end. He passed seagulls and vultures hovering in the air, and they all looked worried.

Smack! Flump!

He landed on his backside. Jonny checked his legs. No sign of anything broken. Incredible! He bounded up and leapt into the air. He leapt higher than he'd ever done before and hovered there for a moment as if he didn't need to land. Then flump! He dropped onto the sand again. Flump! The Fog Prince landed neatly beside him.

Chapter Five

'What else shall we make?' said Jonny as they sat there on the beach.

'Think of a rabbit,' said the prince.

Jonny did and one went hopping past. The Fog Prince caught it by the tail and tickled it under the chin. The rabbit's mouth dropped open and the Fog Prince reached inside.

'Ta dah!' said the Fog Prince and he pulled a bright green hat out. 'Look,' he said, 'I pulled a hat out of a rabbit!'

He handed the hat to Jonny. Jonny heard a mooing sound. He tipped up the hat and four miniature cows fell out, followed by three bears, fourteen baby lambs and some lions. They quickly expanded to full size and went romping away, playing a sort of animal tag. These were then followed by Shimmersteel, Rocktail and Firebreath Slimetongue. Small at first then growing to their normal size. Jonny held up the hat.

'How'd they all get in there?' he asked.

'I'd stand back if I were you,' said the Fog Prince and he made Jonny drop the hat and he pulled him away from it.

There was the sound of thundering feet and a herd of elephants came pouring out of the hat blowing their trunks in terror... followed by a single smiling mouse.

'Elephants don't like mice,' said the prince.

A huge cloud of multi-coloured fog then poured from the hat and broke up into separate shapes, which then became lots of things as they swirled around. Some lolloped slowly past them like sleepy giraffes. Others whizzed by like fast moving trains, speeding along a technicolour track.

'Keep thinking of animals,' called the prince, over the noise of the animal's feet.

Jonny thought for a long time – and with every new thought came a new form of animal, some tiny, some massive. Some ran in circles around him, panting and looking like his school friends spinning on a roundabout, others went back and forth as if they were on elastic, pinging all over the place. Everywhere he looked there were things going on.

'It would be funny if one of those coloured clouds looked like my dad,' he said and there it was. His dad, looking like a bright purple cloud with a huge belly. It seemed there was nothing Jonny couldn't conjure up. He snapped his fingers and his dad and his huge purple belly disappeared.

Eventually Jonny sat down, thought of a cool never ending glass of chocolate and banana milk and drank some of it down. The glass immediately filled back up to the brim. While he drank some more he had an idea. He'd rather not be alone in this world – it would be better to have a few friends around, then they could help him make lots of new things. Maybe they could think up some new things for themselves. Now, he thought, what sort of friends would be good?

Friends he could trust, friends who liked playing and making stuff, friends who would like this new world he'd made, friends who got on well with each other. Friends he could keep. That was important, friends who wouldn't just run off and leave him on his own whenever they felt like it. Great, that's what he'd do. He wandered down to the beach and sat on the yellow sand and began drawing pictures of people with a stick. Normally he wasn't that good at drawing but it seemed to be easier in this new world. He could make his fingers draw what he saw in his head, and before he knew it he'd drawn another person in the sand, a full size boy like himself. A bit shorter than him and with slightly longer hair, but it looked a lot like Jonny. It was a bit like looking in a golden, sandy mirror.

'Sit up,' Jonny whispered, and to his amazement the drawing in the sand sat up.

'Wow!' said Jonny, and he walked all around the new boy.

He looked like a sandy statue, sitting on the beach with his knees pulled up to his chest and his hands pressed each side of him on the ground. Jonny put his face very close to the boy's, his eyes weren't blinking and he didn't look like he was breathing at all.

'Stand up!' said Jonny and the boy did just that, standing to attention like a soldier outside an army barracks.

Jonny walked all around the boy a second time, he was just perfect, and he looked like a statue of Jonny himself.

'Walk,' said Jonny.

The boy took a step.

'Keep walking,' said Jonny.

And the boy took some more steps.

'Go round in a circle,' said Jonny, and he did.

It was like having a remote control robot that didn't need batteries or a remote control. Jonny could just think of something and say it and the boy did it.

'Run really fast,' he said, and the boy sped off, much faster than Jonny had ever run. He might well win the school 100 metres going that fast.

'Come back!' Jonny yelled as the boy disappeared into the distance.

Jonny was worried the boy might not be able to hear him, he'd run so far away, but the boy immediately turned around and zoomed back, stopping right in front of Jonny.

The funny thing was the boy was still not blinking and wasn't out of breath at all. In fact, he still wasn't breathing. He was exactly like a robot.

Jonny snapped his fingers in front of the boy's face but no – he still did not blink.

'What's your name?' said Jonny.

The boy said nothing.

'Hmm, perhaps that's my job,' thought Jonny. 'What should I call you, Zebedee? Speedy? Roadrunner?'

This was difficult.

'I can't think what to call you…'

The boy said nothing.

'What food do you like?' Jonny asked.

The boy said nothing.

'What's your favourite colour?'

Still nothing.

'Do you like James Bond? Harry Potter? Tintin? Sport? Science? Maths? Making stuff?'

Nothing.

This wasn't like any friend Jonny had had before. Sometimes he'd argued with his friends and they had ignored him. ('Coventry-ed him,' they called it.) But that was because they'd had an argument about something. This boy was like no one else Jonny had ever met before.

Chapter Six

Jonny collapsed, lay on the sand and looked up at the sky, it was no longer bright blue as it had been all day. Now it was turning to dark red as the sun was starting to drop down, disappearing behind the sea.

'Must be tea time,' he said, 'are you hungry?'

The boy didn't move.

'This is boring,' said Jonny. 'Say something.'

'Some-thing.'

Jonny jumped. The boy had spoken. But it really did sound like a robot talking.

'What's your name?'

The boy said nothing again.

'Say a joke,' said Jonny.

'A-joke.' said the boy.

'No! Don't just say "a joke". Say something funny,' said Jonny.

'Some-thing-funn-y.'

Jonny didn't laugh.

Neither did the boy, he just stared straight ahead, still not blinking.

'Oh! This is stupid!' said Jonny. 'Sit down and have a rest. I'm going for some tea.'

The boy sat down, pulled his knees up to his chest and stared out to sea, and he still did not blink. Jonny went off for some food and a long think. He picked some bananas, berries and dates and found a pool full of fresh orange juice. The food tasted like nothing on earth - which was sort of true really. Earth was somewhere else beyond Jonny's dream. Eventually he strolled slowly back. The boy was still sitting, knees pulled to his chest, eyes wide. Jonny walked around him one way then back the other, and slowly the penny dropped. It made a kerching! sound in his mind.

'You're like a robot aren't you?' Jonny said and the boy nodded. 'you can do anything as long as I make it happen.'

The boy nodded again.

'Hmm,' said Jonny and he sat opposite the boy in the cool evening. He pulled his knees up to his chest and looked like a mirror image of him. He took a big decision. 'Okaayyyyy...' Jonny said slowly, 'I want you to live. Be alive! But - you must do everything I say. I'm in charge.'

The boy didn't move. 'I-am-a-live,' he said, still in his metallic robot voice.

Jonny jumped up and kicked the sand. 'But you're not! You're no fun.'

Jonny paced up and down. He liked having a boy he could boss around, but not like this. He sat down opposite the boy again.

'Right, listen to me,' said Jonny, 'there are lots of things to do here. We can make an awesome world here. What I want you to do is think of lots of new things we can do together and any new things we can invent. Get it?'

The boy nodded but didn't move.

'Okay then,' said Jonny. 'You're free to think for yourself. Stop being a robot.'

'Are-you-sure?' said the boy and it made Jonny jump back a little.

'Yes. No. Yes. No. Yes.' He thought for a moment. 'I think so. Yes! Be free! Go on!'

The boy blinked. And then blinked again. And then he smiled. It was the first time he'd looked happy.

'Hello,' he said.

'Hello, I'm Jonny,' said Jonny, it was like they were meeting for the first time.

The boy looked around, opened his eyes wide and said, 'Wow!' and he really meant it.

Jonny and the boy made lots of things together. New plants, trees, wild animals, tame animals, insects, fish, fruit, games, birds, comics, jokes, words they barely understood, wasps for which they could think of no real purpose, sweets that did you no damage and plenty of other extraordinary creations. The inventions went on and on. They high-fived each other when each great new idea appeared and laughed loudly at the weird shapes of some of the fish and birds. At one point Rocktail, Shimmersteel and Firebreath Slimetongue came and joined in, or got in the way, depending on how you looked at the situation.

'What do you think you're doing?'

Jonny turned to the familiar voice. It was the Fog Prince, he was standing looking at Jonny and the boy. But he wasn't looking happy. His hands were on his hips and there was a scowl on his face. 'What do you think you're doing?' he said again.

'Having fun. Where've you been?'

The Fog Prince didn't reply, instead he walked closer and studied the boy.

'Who's this?'

'My new friend. I made him, well, I thought of him and he appeared. Say hello.'

The Fog Prince stood right in front of the boy, looked him up and down slowly and then said a quiet, 'Hello, you.'

The boy felt a shiver run through him for the first time. 'H...ello,' he said.

'This is my friend,' said Jonny, 'the Fog Prince.'

'I'm his best friend,' said the Fog Prince.

'Yes. Sort of,' said Jonny.

The Fog Prince turned and stared at Jonny.

'What do you mean - sort of?' he demanded.

'Well, I have lots of friends don't I?'

'But I showed you everything here. I explained it all. I helped you. To make things.'

'Yes, and now I've made the boy. And he's a new friend. I'm thinking about making a girl too.'

'A girl?' the boy and the Fog Prince said at the same time, and both of their eyebrows shot up high on their foreheads.

Jonny laughed. 'Yes, if we have a boy we should have a girl.'

The boy and the Fog Prince looked worried.

'Is that wise?' said the Fog Prince.

Jonny shrugged. 'Why not?' And he snapped his fingers.

The boy dropped in a heap on the floor. He started snoring quietly.

'Take out a rib,' said Jonny.

'You take out a rib,' said the prince, it was the first time he had disagreed with Jonny.

'Why won't you do it?' said Jonny.

'It'll be messy. And I don't want to.'

Jonny shrugged, bent down and grabbed at the boy's side. There was a loud crack and a squelching sound. The Fog Prince sucked his breath in, the boy groaned and sighed then snored again. Jonny stood up and held up a bit of bone. 'Not messy at all,' he said.

Jonny stepped away and placed the bone on the ground. Then he closed his eyes and hummed to himself happily. As the Fog Prince watched the bone grew other bones and then sinews and muscles appeared, and then skin. It all happened quite quickly. Jonny opened his eyes.

'There we go,' he said with a smile. 'A girl!'

The girl did not look like the boy. She looked more like Jonny's cousin Ruth. Brown hair, a few freckles, a roundish kind of face, a tiny dimple on her chin. She opened her eyes, saw Jonny and smiled.

'Hello,' she said, 'who are you?'

She sat up as she said it and held out her hand.

Jonny took it, thinking she wanted to shake his hand, but instead she grabbed it and pulled herself onto her feet. Then she turned and looked at the boy, still lying asleep on the ground, and said, 'Wow!'

This woke the boy up, and he turned, saw her, scrambled to his feet and leapt back, all in just a few seconds. He looked amazed and a little bit terrified. Then he winced and glanced down at his rib cage. He rubbed it for a moment then pointed to the girl.

'Look what I made,' said Jonny. 'Like her?'

'Her?' said the boy.

'Yes, remember I said I was going to make a girl? This is what they look like.'

The boy walked round her and rubbed his chin.

The Fog Prince shook his head. 'This can only mean trouble,' he said.

'This can only mean more ideas,' Jonny corrected him. 'She'll make up things we could never have thought about.'

The Fog Prince backed away and watched from a distance. The boy and the girl began talking. She said something that was obviously funny because the boy and Jonny laughed. The Fog Prince frowned. This was all getting out of hand. He walked away slowly, with the sound of their laughter still ringing in his ears.

'What is this place? What can we do here?' asked the girl as the Fog Prince moved further away.

'You decide,' said Jonny, 'I'm not making all the decisions. You make some too.'

'What do you mean?' asked the girl.

'Well, for one thing you can pick your own names, and decide what food you like and what to do every day.'

The boy looked shocked. 'But we want you to tell us what to do.'

'No, I'm changing things – you can decide. I want to see what things you make up. It'll be more fun. Honest.'

'I want to be Julie-Tilda-Florence-Madge,' said the girl.

'What?' said Jonny and the boy.

'My name. I want to be Julie-Tilda-Florence-Madge. I like that. What about you two?'

'I'm Jonny,' said Jonny.

'I don't know,' said the boy.

The girl smiled. 'You could be Sludge-Slurry-Transit-Van,' she said and she laughed.

The boy looked confused. 'That's a stoopid name,' he said shaking his head.

'Then think of a better one,' she said happily. 'So,' she said to Jonny. 'We can make up anything?'

'Anything,' said Jonny, 'I've decided, and if I've decided, then it happens.'

'Wow!' said the girl, and she looked suddenly excited. She opened her eyes wide and looked round, turning in a circle. She began to run and skip and jump. The boy ran to catch up with her. They crouched down in the sand together, whispered, laughed, then grabbed handfuls of sand, threw them up in the air and blew at them. The golden grains hovered for a moment before fizzing like a clutch of tiny fireworks, then exploding into a cloud of brightly coloured wings. The wings became butterflies and the butterflies flickered around the boy and girl.

The girl cupped one in her hand, and peeked at it through the gap between her palms.

'This place is beautiful,' she said and Jonny grinned.

It is, he thought. I've made something really cool. Really awesome. I think I like it.

He watched as the boy and girl chased after the butterflies, closely followed by Rocktail and Shimmersteel. Then he heard a faint hissing noise and turned to see the Fog Prince standing in the distance. He was holding something, playing with a long thin creature as it wound round his arms and neck. He must have made something new. Jonny went to see what it was.

Chapter Seven

'I'm thinking of making a new world,' said the Fog Prince.

Jonny was sitting cross-legged on the beach, drawing in the sand. The Fog Prince was standing next to him. The sun was coming up, it was just breaking dawn.

'I'm tired of this one,' said the prince.

Jonny looked up sharply. 'Tired of this one? How can you be tired, it's brilliant. Plus, we've only just started. Who needs another world? There's plenty going on here.'

The Fog Prince sighed.

'I know,' he said, 'but... well it's different now, isn't it?'

'Different?'

'Yes. Since you did that thing without me.'

'What thing?' asked Jonny.

'You know, you made those two strange creatures.'

Jonny grinned. 'You mean the boy and the girl. I love 'em, they're awesome.'

'But you gave them too much. You should have made them more like that dragon and the unicorn you like so much.'

'Rocktail and Shimmersteel?'

'Yes. You didn't tell them they could make anything they wanted. And you didn't... well... make them look like - you. You really should have consulted me first, you know.'

'I took... er... an executive decision,' said Jonny, though he only had half an idea about what an executive decision was. He'd heard his dad use the phrase a few times.

'Well I don't like it,' muttered the prince. 'You spoilt this place.'

Jonny looked at the Fog Prince carefully. He looked a little different somehow. Not anything you could put your finger on, just... different. And he had that long, thin, green creature with him. It never stopped slithering up and down his arm and round his neck. Always slithering, never stopping.

'You want to be careful that slimy thing doesn't strangle you,' said Jonny, as a sort of joke.

The Fog Prince laughed, but not in a happy kind of way. 'With those two creatures you made you'll have to be careful of lots of things,' he replied and he turned and began to walk away.

'What will you do in your new world?' Jonny asked.

'Anything I like.'

'But you can do that here, in my world.'

The prince looked back and laughed again. 'No Jonny. You can't. You have to do what the boy and girl want to do. You gave them the run of the place, remember?'

Jonny watched him walk away and thought for a while, it wasn't supposed to be like this. Not in his new amazing world. He called out to the prince. 'You're just jealous, 'cause I made them without you,' said Jonny.

The Fog Prince didn't look back, he merely shrugged his shoulders and walked on. The green creature looked at him though, over the prince's shoulder. Its tongue snaked out towards Jonny, like it was insulting him.

The girl was sunbathing. When she opened her eyes he was looking down at her. The Fog Prince. He had a long restless green creature wrapped around his neck and draped down his arm.

'Nice here, isn't it?' he said.

She nodded and smiled.

'I love it,' she said.

'Where's the boy?' asked the prince.

She shrugged. 'Off building something, or messing about with Rocktail and the others. I said I'd take a break, I spent all morning designing a duck-billed-razorback-pot-bellied velocer-rex. What about you? Nothing to do?'

The Fog Prince shook his head. 'I have plenty to do,' he said.

The girl closed her eyes and they stayed in silence for a moment.

'D'you like Jonny?' the prince asked after a while.

'Of course,' she said, as if there was really no other possibility.

'He's kind of bossy though, isn't he?' said the prince.

She frowned. 'Bossy?'

'You know, always telling you what to do.'

She shook her head and sat up. 'No, he's just the opposite, he's always asking us for help.'

The Fog Prince sniffed. 'Same thing really isn't it. Won't leave you in peace.'

'I have plenty of peace,' she said.

'Fair enough,' said the Fog Prince and he began to stroll away. He stopped and looked back. 'I thought I might start my own new world. Wanna come?'

'What?'

'Well Jonny's got this place all worked out now, and you and the boy have invented plenty of things for it. I thought I'd start again. I could use your help.'

She scratched her head. This was an odd idea, it kind of opened up her mind in a new way.

'What would Jonny say?'

'Oh he won't mind. Don't mention it though, I plan to build it and surprise him.'

Surprise Jonny? That was a new idea. Not mentioning something.... hmm... that thought had never entered her head before.

'Is it okay to not mention something to Jonny?' she asked and the Fog Prince laughed.

'Of course, he said, 'I do it all the time and I'm okay aren't I?'

He walked back to her and knelt down so he could whisper in her ear.

'Jonny likes surprises. And he did say he wanted you and the boy to do anything you wanted.'

She could hear the gentle hissing of the green creature as the Fog Prince spoke. She felt its tongue flick at her cheek.

The Fog Prince straightened up and began to walk away again.

'Just think,' he said as he went, 'a whole new world of possibilities.' He stopped one more time to look back at her. 'And I'd be looking for a queen to rule it. Think about it.'

And he went. But she did think about it, the idea danced around her mind for the rest of the day. And when the others came back from their antics there was something delicious about letting the idea run around her mind without the others knowing it was even there at all.

The next day she let the others go off inventing and exploring while she stayed back sunbathing again. She lay around a whole day, but the Fog Prince didn't appear again. When the others came back she felt another new emotion - frustration. She didn't mention this to the others, but she didn't feel happy towards them at all. The next day she made another excuse and wandered off to a nearby river to distract herself by designing a few new fish. She was leaning over studying the water when she felt the tap on the shoulder.

It was the Fog Prince. He was back.

'Want to go for a walk?' he said.

'I thought you weren't coming back,' said the girl.

'I always keep my word,' said the prince and he offered her his hand.

She took it and stood up and walked with him. He had the green creature again, slithering up and down his arm. Hissing as it went.

They walked for a while until they came to a door standing in the middle of nowhere. There was no frame to it, no hinges, no walls around it. Just a door standing there with nothing to do.

'Oh but this has plenty to do,' said the Fog Prince, as if he was reading her mind. 'Just push it.'

She started to reach towards it then something held her back, as if there was an invisible arm tugging at hers, stopping her from opening the door.

'What's the problem?' said the prince. 'Just push it.'

She reached out a second time and once again she pulled back, feeling that tug on her arm.

'It won't bite,' said the prince and he laughed, but it wasn't a kind sort of laugh.

She reached again, and this time when the tugging came she was prepared and ignored it. She just pushed on and her hand pressed against the wood. It was oddly cold, like someone had kept it in a freezer for a while. She thought her hand might get stuck to it, but no, the door gave a gentle click and swung open.

'Take a look,' said the prince and he pushed her towards it a little.

She leant forward to look, frightened that she might fall down some invisible hole. Beyond the door there was the sound of laughter and music and chattering. She went closer. Through the door there were all kinds of strange colours swirling around. The more she watched them the more she wanted to reach out and touch them. It was mesmerising. She took another step... and the door slammed suddenly in her face, making her jump back with shock.

'It wouldn't be fair to go through on your own,' said the Fog Prince.

'What do you mean?' the girl looked at her outstretched hand, it was shaking with a mixture of excitement and nervousness.

'Well if you're going to make a new world for Jonny you should bring the boy too.'

She thought about this for a moment.

'Well, maybe I could just take a look first.'

The Fog Prince snapped his fingers and the door vanished. It was gone. She felt another mixed feeling, relief and disappointment.

'No,' said the prince, putting a hand on her shoulder and steering her away from the spot where the door had been. 'You get the boy and we'll do this together.'

'When? When will we do this together?'

He smiled. 'Soon,' he said and he snapped his fingers and melted into thin air.

Chapter Eight

She knew what she had to do, of course. The Fog Prince hadn't said it in so many words, but somehow she had to persuade the boy to go and explore this new world with her. She found him riding Rocktail, with Jonny on Shimmersteel. They were jumping boulders, bushes and low trees, on their way to nowhere in particular. She sat high up at a distance and watched them cavorting about in a place they had called the Valley of Sweet Water. The valley was full of little brooks, each one carrying a different flavoured water. She was thirsty but didn't want to go down. She wanted to catch the boy alone, when Jonny wasn't around, so she sat hunched up in the shadow of a jagged rock, her throat dry and her face hot.

At one point they jumped off the animals and sat making elaborate boats out of shells and leaves and bits of twigs, she could hear them laughing in the distance, talking about things as they worked. Eventually they finished and let the boats go bobbing down one of the wider brooks. The boy punched the air as he saw his boat overtake Jonny's. It wasn't a race but it was great to be winning anyway. In the background, beyond the boats in the brook, Rocktail and Shimmersteel were engaged in some sort of bout for supremacy. Rocktail was swinging his mighty tail and throwing his extra weight against the unicorn, Shimmersteel was using his horn as a battering ram against Rocktail's chest and backside. The girl thought it would never end and she was just about to slip away when Jonny stood up, stretched and said something to the boy. Then he ran and jumped on Shimmersteel and pounded off in a cloud of dust. This was her chance.

'Whatcha doing?' she asked, approaching the boy with gentle footsteps.

The boy looked up, he smiled and held up his boat. He had added tiny silver silk ropes to the sail on it.

'Look what I made!' he said, holding up the boat, 'and it's faster than Jonny's.'

Rocktail came over and nuzzled his huge snout against her back, she shooed him away.

'I've found a new world,' she said.

He frowned. 'We've already got one,' he replied.

She laughed and shook her head.

'This one's better.'

'How can it be better? We can do anything here.'

'It's bigger, brighter, funnier.'

The boy frowned, he had no idea what she was talking about. She grabbed at his shoulder, tugged at him to follow her.

'Honest,' she said, 'come with me and I'll show you.'

Rocktail started to follow but she shooed him away again.

She took him back to the spot where the-door-with-no-frame had been standing. It was visible again. Just waiting there in the middle of nowhere. There was no sign of the Fog Prince though, just the door.

'Look, see?' she said. 'A magic door.'

She pressed her hand against it and pushed it open. It swung wide and once again the girl heard the laughter and chatter from the world on the other side. And this time the boy heard it too. His eyes widened.

'What's going on in there?' he asked.

'Let's go in and find out,' said the girl.

There was an ear-bashing, thundering sound and a rush of cold air as they stepped through the doorway. The space swelled like a cartoon door to allow them both to pass through at the same time. The boy shivered.

'What was that noise?' he asked.

'Oh probably just a draught from one world to another,' said the girl. 'Come on, let's get exploring.'

They spent the day there. And no one really knows what they found, invented, created or discovered, but when they came back through that doorway their eyes were wide and their hair was sticking up in spiky patterns.

The Fog Prince was standing there waiting by the door when they returned to Jonny's world.

'See,' said the Fog Prince. 'Pretty awesome eh?'

They nodded silently. And then the boy shivered again.

'I think I'll just go a for a swim,' he said and the girl agreed and without saying goodbye they left the prince and wandered over to a nearby lake where the water was sweet and warm. They said nothing as they jumped in and splashed about.

Chapter Nine

Jonny was enjoying himself.

He'd never been that good at art, or creating things at school, he had recently got 8 out of 100 in an art exam, but here it seemed that didn't matter, he could do anything. Back at Dagenham Drive he often felt awkward and clumsy. But not here. Here he was in charge. The only blip was his argument with the Fog Prince. Why they had argued he didn't really know, and it had hardly been an argument really, but he wasn't happy about it. This wasn't a world for falling out with others. That was in the other world. The world where he lived with his parents and his Star Wars lamp, where he messed about with his friends, and sometimes argued with them.

Where were the boy and the girl? He hadn't seen them for a while. That was strange. He wandered around their favourite haunts. He spotted Rocktail dozing in the shade of a rock, came across Shimmersteel basking in the sun, and almost tripped over Firebreath Slimetongue hiding under a massive bush. But there was no sign of the boy or girl.

He walked on for a while until something fell out of the sky. It was a huge piece of rock and it almost hit him. It landed right beside him and he had to leap out of the way. Then the ground in front of him shook a little and a crack appeared as the ground split, like tearing two bits of pizza apart. Strands of loose earth hung between the gap like stringy cheese but there was no great pizza smell. In fact the gap smelt very bad indeed. Smoke rose up and there was a smell like a rotten egg or a stink bomb, or the kitchen bin when it hadn't been emptied for three weeks. Something was happening. Something strange. Jonny looked back, turned round and went back to Firebreath Slimetongue. He tapped on his nose, hoping the dragon wouldn't belch out a huge flame of fire in surprise. The dragon opened a huge golden eye.

'Why are you hiding?' Jonny asked him.

'I'm not,' said Firebreath Slimetongue, but he wasn't telling the truth and Jonny could see it.

'What's going on?' he asked.

Firebreath Slimetongue sat up and sighed, which was a big mistake because he almost toasted Jonny with the flames from his nose.

'Oops, sorry,' he said in his strange high-pitched voice. He looked over at Rocktail nearby.

Jonny noticed for the first time that Rocktail had a scowl on his face. He never scowled.

Shimmersteel didn't look so happy either. He had some scratches on his fantastic horn.

'They had a fight,' said Firebreath Slimetongue.

'But they always tussle,' said Jonny.

'This wasn't a tussle,' said Firebreath Slimetongue, 'they got really angry. Rocktail's hurt.'

Jonny hurried over to him, the dinosaur had a wound on his left side. He groaned when Jonny ran his hand over it.

'This wasn't supposed to happen,' said Jonny, 'I made us all to be friends.'

'Well something's changed, ' said Firebreath Slimetongue as he came over, 'and I don't like it.'

Jonny turned and looked across his new land. In the distance dark clouds were skulking on the horizon, intending to creep across the sky towards them like an angry giant. Behind him Rocktail groaned in pain, nearby Shimmersteel made a face and rubbed his damaged horn in the dirt. Firebreath looked even more miserable. Something was very wrong indeed.

Jonny left Rocktail, Shimmersteel and Firebreath behind and went in search of the boy and girl. Before long a tall, dark figure appeared in the distance. He looked familiar but he also looked different. Jonny narrowed his eyes and tried to see who it was, but the clouds overhead made it dark and difficult to see. He walked on. Slowly he realised, it was the Fog Prince, but he certainly looked a little strange. He had changed, he was darker in colour, the gold, silver and scarlet had tarnished and was looking rusty now. As he walked his large body rattled and crackled and thundered as if it was made of storm clouds. He held up his hand and his thick fingers looked like foamy grey sausages.

'Far enough,' he said.

Jonny stopped.

'What do you mean, far enough?' he asked. He really didn't understand.

'I made a new world,' said the Fog Prince. 'It's fantastic. The boy and girl are the king and queen.'

'Is that where they are?' asked Jonny.

The Fog Prince grinned, and thick wisps of smoky, smoggy breath slipped out of his mouth.

'Don't bother looking for them,' said the Fog Prince, 'they're on my side now.'

'What do you mean - they're on your side now?'

The Fog Prince laughed. 'Stop saying "what do you mean" and then repeating what I just said. Are you an idiot?'

Jonny didn't understand, this was all going wrong. This was his world, not the Fog Prince's. He decided to tell the prince this.

'It's my world, not yours,' he said, but the Fog Prince just laughed again.

'You can have this world. I've got a better one.'

'But you can't just take the boy and girl, they're my friends.'

'Not any more. They're my friends now.'

Jonny felt a sudden shiver run through his body.

At the same time the Fog Prince raised his hand and snapped his finger.

There was a terrible sound in the sky, a mixture of thunder and screaming and a horrible kind of laughter. The ground shook so much that Jonny fell over. When he looked up grey misty figures were starting to appear in rows behind the Fog Prince. They were tall and dark and cloudy like the prince. They looked a little familiar.

'Remember this lot?' said the prince.

Jonny looked a little closer. He was still sitting on the floor.

They were the helpers he had made not so long ago, but they had changed, just like the Fog Prince had. They weren't bright and colourful any more.

'This is my army now,' said the prince, 'and we're off to my world. And there's nothing you can do.'

Jonny jumped up, he wasn't standing for this. He clapped his hands. A crowd of foggy figures appeared around him, pulsating with colour and light.

'I'm still in charge,' said Jonny, 'and this is my army.'

But the Fog Prince laughed.

Then the rest of his grey misty army laughed too, and the sound was dreadful. Cackling, shrieking, nothing happy about it at all. Jonny and his friends just watched and waited for the others to quieten again. Eventually, when the Fog Prince raised his arms, they did all shut up.

'Don't mess with me, Jonny,' said the prince, 'you don't want that kind of trouble.'

'I just want the boy and the girl back,' said Jonny. 'That's what I want. Now where are they?'

The Fog Prince looked Jonny up and down once. Just the once. Then suddenly his eyes flashed a dirty yellow and he roared with his smoky, smoggy breath and something terrible happened. Something Jonny could not quite work out. He just felt it in his bones. The Fog Prince drew himself up to his full height and his whole body and face changed. He became terrible and horrible and frightening all at once in a way that was impossible to describe or understand. Then the rest of his army joined in and Jonny's world turned dark as they changed shape into huge hideous foggy shapes. Behind them, against the dark skyline, a mountain split open and fire and smoke exploded from the top.

Jonny took a step back and the rest of his friends did the same. They turned as they heard the sound of thundering steps, pounding towards them. It was Firebreath Slimetongue and Shimmersteel. The two huge creatures skidded to a halt, their feet kicking up clouds of dust and dirt. Firebreath stood near to Jonny, but Shimmersteel shook his head and went and stood on the side of the Fog Prince. There was no sign of Rocktail. The two sides looked at each other and no one moved.

Chapter Ten

No one was quite sure who moved first. It might have been a nervous twitch from Firebreath, or maybe Shimmersteel got an itch on his damaged horn and rubbed it in the dirt. Or perhaps one of the Fog Prince's army got trigger happy. Whichever way someone moved and suddenly the two armies piled into each other. You might find it hard to imagine that fog bodies could really do anything to each other, being made of such thin misty stuff, but they knew how to hurt and damage each other. Bodies grappled and swirled around and flew broken against nearby rocks. Firebreath and Shimmersteel smashed foreheads and butted each other again and again and again. They must have both got quite a headache. The Fog Prince himself opened his mouth and poured a foul-smelling smoggy cloud of breath all over Jonny, and while Jonny was coughing and spluttering the prince lifted him up on one hand and threw him against a nearby tree. As Jonny and the cloud of breath came into contact with the tree the branches curled up and the leaves withered and began to drop. The Fog Prince left him and continued to saunter about, picking up the bright pulsating figures in Jonny's army, covering them in his foul breath and smashing them into bushes and flowers and trees. And wherever they landed things began to die. The Fog Prince and his dark army were winning. Jonny's friends were doing their best but the others were overpowering them.

The battle raged on. Jonny's multi-coloured fog knights fought hard, and every time they got knocked down they got right back up and waded into the battle again. The Fog Prince's sneering, leering troops celebrated every time they picked up another of Jonny's friends and hurled them against a tree. They belched smoke and spit and pulled incredibly disgusting faces. At one point they turned to each other, formed a large circle and gave each other a huge group high five. Beyond them the dark mountain in the distance spewed fire again. Jonny took the chance to withdraw a little and re-gather his men.

'Look, ' he said, 'we can't win this, they're too powerful. What can we do?'

He looked around the group of coloured, battered faces. There was no blood, fog soldiers didn't bleed, but there were plenty of multi-coloured scrapes and bruises among them.

'They must have a weakness,' said Jonny.

'They do,' said a voice.

Jonny looked across the group to where the gravelly sounding voice had come from.

A tall, strong figure stepped towards him. The fog soldier glowed a little brighter than the others.

'You Jonny,' he said, 'you're their weakness.'

'Me?' Jonny blinked a couple of times as he said this.

The tall figure nodded. He spoke slowly and quietly, unrushed, even though the Fog Prince's army was turning round again, getting ready for another attack.

'This is still your world Jonny. While we fight like this we are playing their game. They're taking control. This isn't the way you made things. You know that Jonny, don't you?'

Behind the tall figure the dark sneering friends of the Fog Prince were starting to move closer again, Jonny could hear them spitting and snarling.

'Don't panic Jonny, don't take any notice of them. Think. You created all this. What do you want us to do?'

An idea suddenly crashed into Jonny's mind. He remembered how it had all begun with himself and the fog people making loads of things. He glanced around and was shocked at the flowers and trees that were dying all over his world. The fight with the Fog Prince's army was killing them.

'Make new stuff,' he said suddenly.

His army frowned and scratched their brightly coloured heads.

'What?'

'Make some new things,' said Jonny. 'Look! Those things you made before are dying.'

The tall figure studied Jonny's face for a moment then slowly he nodded and dropped to his knees. He scooped up a handful of scuffed earth and breathed on it. A new fragile plant began to grow up in his palm. He dug a little hole and placed the plant in it. The rest of Jonny's army gathered round to watch. Behind them the Fog Prince's men had no idea what was happening. But they kept coming closer, snarling and spitting as they came.

Chapter Eleven

As the tall figure knelt in the dirt, planting the new flower he'd made, the Fog Prince's men closed in. The brightly coloured warriors of Jonny's army could feel the foul, hot breath of their enemies burning on their necks. The Fog Prince shouted something and his men sneered as one and raised their arms to grab Jonny's friends. But before they could take hold Jonny's men dropped to a kneeling position and began scooping up handfuls of dirt. They breathed on them and began to mould them into newly shaped creations. Their hands were shaking a little but they ignored the spitting and the threats from the dark army leering behind them. Only Jonny was standing, surrounded by kneeling figures. And as his friends concentrated on creating new things they glowed brighter than before and the Fog Prince's men had to lift their gnarled fingers to shield their eyes from the brightness.

Jonny looked up and across at the Fog Prince. He was frowning. His face all cloudy and angry.

'Tell them to get up and fight!' he yelled, spitting smoke as he said it.

But Jonny just looked at him and slowly shook his head.

Jonny's friends glowed brighter still as they crouched and worked, and soon the ground around them was full of fresh plants and bushes, new creatures and coloured insects. The sound of squeaking and chirping was beginning to fill the air. The prince's men looked confused, their clawed hands were grabbing at the air above the kneeling figures, as if they were still expecting to take hold of Jonny's men. The Fog Prince raised his blackened hand and pointed it hard at Jonny. The fingers were shaking, not from fear, but anger.

'You... you... you'll pay for this,' he said, bits of dirty spit coming out with the words, 'this... this is not the end. You have not won. You will never win. This may be your world, but I have my own.' He jabbed his finger at his chest, then he jabbed it back at Jonny, the finger nail was long and sharp and jagged. 'And you will never - never - enter it. I forbid it. Say goodbye to that miserable boy and girl you made, their life is over. You hear me? OVER!' He yelled the last word, and slashed at the air with his jagged finger as if to underline it. Then he turned on his heel and left, trailing a streak of grey smoke behind him as he stormed away.

One by one the men of his army realised they should go too and they gave up attempting to grab at Jonny's friends. Instead they turned and shuffled away, doing their best to catch up with the Fog Prince. Jonny sighed and collapsed onto the ground. He felt really tired after the battle and that last encounter with the Fog Prince. He also felt very sad too. The prince had been his friend. He felt something on his hand and looked down. A tiny blue grasshopper had landed on his finger and was making a gentle, buzzing kind of humming noise. A small rabbit was butting his foot with its nose. Jonny smiled and looked around at his friends, they were doing a great job, still creating new things.

'Well done,' he said quietly. 'You did it.'

The tall figure stepped up and crouched beside him. Even crouching down he was taller than Jonny.

'Well done you,' he said. 'You did it too Jonny.'

He put a big hand on Jonny's shoulder and squeezed it to encourage him.

'I'm gonna call you Dook Strong,' said Jonny, 'I think I'm gonna need you.'

He probably meant Duke Strong, but he pronounced it Dook, and Dook just nodded.

'We'll figure out something,' the big man said with a smile.

He stood up again. 'Now then,' he said, 'what are we going to do with all these new creatures?'

There were so many rabbits, moles, mice and guinea pigs running amok, you had to be very careful not to tread on one.

Chapter Twelve

They spent the rest of the day transporting the new creatures to new nests and burrows around the place, and transplanting new plants and bushes to the places where the Fog Prince and his men had caused devastation in the battle. At the end of the day the other fog friends disappeared into the cool night, leaving Jonny and Dook Strong sitting around a camp fire. The place was cooler since the Fog Prince had changed things. Many of the dark clouds overhead had blown away but there were still a few gloomy patches in the sky.

'Something affected the Fog Prince,' Dook Strong said.

Jonny nodded. 'He seemed to get upset about me making the boy and the girl. He didn't like that.'

Jonny squeezed a chocolate and banana marshmallow onto a stick and held it over the fire. The edges turned brown and bubbly.

'Envy,' said Dook Strong, nodding to himself. 'It happens. He got jealous of you having other friends, Jonny. He wanted to keep you for himself.'

Jonny shrugged. 'That's crazy. I still wanted to be friends with him.'

Dook Strong shrugged. 'I guess it's too late now,' he said, 'his whole body turned into a storm cloud. You saw him. Not good at all.'

They sat in silence for a minute while Jonny chewed on his cooked marshmallow.

'I have to find the boy and the girl,' Jonny said, picking a few stringy bits of marshmallow off his chin.

'I'll scout about tomorrow and see what I can find out,' said Dook Strong.

He put his big hand on Jonny's shoulder. 'For now though, I suggest you sleep. You've had a tough day.'

Jonny curled up by the fire and watched the flames dancing around. He wondered if he might wake up in the morning back in his bed, back in 72 Dagenham Drive. For the first time since his dream had begun he hoped he might. At some point he fell asleep.

It was morning. His Star Wars lamp was by his bed. There was no burnt-out camp fire. No dark clouds in the sky. No sign of Dook Strong. Jonny was back, back home. He sat up. The door began to open, Jonny grinned, it would be his mum with a cup of tea and a smile. A grey hand snaked around the door, the nails long and sharp and jagged. It wasn't his mother at all. It was the Fog Prince. Here in Dagenham Drive. Jonny backed up against the headboard of his bed. He picked up the Star Wars lamp and threw it. Unfortunately it was still plugged in and didn't get anywhere near the leering face of the prince, instead it bounced back and hit Jonny on the head, knocking him out. He fell back and bumped his head on the headboard as he went. He lay still for a few moments.

Then he blinked, and woke up again. He was back. By the burnt-out fire, under that sky, and here was Dook Strong coming to wake him up. At least he had a cup of something steaming in his hand. He passed it to Jonny and he sipped it. It was like tea but not. Sweet. Tasty. Zingy. Different. He drank it down. Afterwards he felt full, as if he'd just eaten a good breakfast.

'I dreamt I was back home,' he said.

Dook nodded. 'You will be,' he said, 'one day.'

He offered Jonny one of his huge hands and lifted him up to standing.

'I'm going for a scout about,' Dook said, his voice was serious and gravelly.

'I'll go and see about the damage from the fight yesterday,' Jonny said.

'Meet back here in a couple of hours,' Dook said and he strode away.

He took big strides and moved quickly. Jonny was pleased Dook Strong was on his side. Relieved too.

It was easy to find the battlefield again. It was surrounded by a ring of trees and plants that were wilting or dead. New plants were already starting to come through the soil and add some green to the brown deadness of the place. But it was still a sad sight. A couple of Jonny's fog friends appeared with rakes and forks and they began sorting out some of the mess. Jonny helped them for a while. Then he spotted something, something which made his blood run cold. A dark mound in the distance. At first he thought it was just a large rock, blackened by yesterday's battle. But as he narrowed his eyes and studied it from a distance the truth hit him. He started to run.

Meanwhile Dook found the door. That strange door standing in the middle of nowhere. No door frame, no hinges. Just a door. He pushed against it and suddenly pulled back his hand. It was hot. Too hot for him to touch. He put his hand in a nearby pool of water and a cloud of steam rose up. He tried to shove the door open with his shoulder but his clothes caught fire and he had to run around beating out the flames for a while. Clearly someone did not want him to go through. A small rabbit hopped up to watch what was going on. Dook picked up a massive handful of dust and threw it at the door. It bounced off in a shower of sparks and the rabbit ran for its life, its tail singed and smoking from the heat. Dook dropped onto his haunches and shoved his huge, craggy, cliff-edge chin into his hands. What could he do?

Jonny walked up to the grey mound he had seen. It was Rocktail, that big friendly lumbering mountain of life. That dinosaur friend of Jonny's. He was lying very still, his tail skewed at an odd angle and the wound in his side flopping open. His body was not rising up and down as it would have done if he was just sleeping in the sun. Jonny knelt down and placed his ear on the hard scaly skin. Nothing. No breath, no heartbeat. Rocktail was dead. The Fog Prince had brought the ultimate problem to Jonny's world. Death. Jonny pulled his head away from Rocktail's chest and sniffed. Loudly. He looked around, he was alone. He wiped the tears from his cheeks and sniffed again. This settled it. He had to do something. As he stood up he heard footsteps pounding towards him, he turned. It was Dook Strong, he was running towards him.

'I found out where...' Dook stopped when he saw Rocktail. He dropped down beside the creature and ran a big hand over his mountainous back. 'Is he gone?'

Jonny nodded. 'Dead,' he said.

Dook nodded too then stood up and rested his hand on Jonny's shoulder.

'You okay?' he asked.

Jonny nodded but didn't say anything.

'I found a door,' said Dook, 'a door to another world.'

Jonny's eyes widened. 'The Fog Prince's world?' he said. 'I bet that's where he's taken the boy and the girl.'

Dook nodded. 'Absolutely. I met the girl at the door.'

'What?'

'I was waiting by the door wondering what to do,' said Dook, 'when I saw it open a little and I caught her peeping through it at me. She said she'd heard someone banging on it. They're trapped in there Jonny. The Fog Prince has fixed it so that we can't open it our side, and they're not allowed to leave their side.'

Jonny began pacing up and down. His feet scuffed the earth as he went, leaving a weave of endless trails. He stopped and raised a finger.

'If she opens the door maybe I can go through,' said Jonny.

'Then what?'

Jonny's face lit up. 'I can get revenge!'

'Is that what you really want? Remember what happened when we tried fighting the Fog Prince and his men.'

'Dook!' Jonny shouted, really angry now. 'I'm in charge. Not him. He may think that's his world beyond the door, but it's all in my world. It's part of what I put together.'

'Sure. But there must be better ways to win this,' said Dook.

Jonny started pacing again. This time he didn't turn round and retrace his steps but he kept walking. Dook watched him stroll into the distance. Eventually, when he was alone, Jonny stopped and looked around.

Chapter Thirteen

It was strange being in a place with no houses or cars. Everywhere Jonny looked he could see for miles. Grass stretching like vast carpets. Trees and bushes all green and speckled, loaded with fruits of all colours, looking fat and juicy and delicious. Birds and creatures sang and squeaked and chirruped all around. Brooks ran with all kinds of flavoured water, and the weather had warmed up and the beach was close by. And the sand there stretched on for miles. An epic, smooth, golden carpet. This was a great place and it gave him the best feeling. He loved it. And he had made it all. He and his new friends. Jonny and the fog people and the boy and the girl. And the Fog Prince. Only now the Fog Prince had turned against him and stolen his friends away. Jonny walked again and thought about this for quite a while.

Dook Strong was raking up the last of the dead leaves when Jonny reappeared with a smile.

I've got a plan,' he said. 'Did you say you'd meet the girl again?'

'I said I'd be there tomorrow about the same time,' said Dook.

He lifted up a massive handful of dead leaves, breathed on them and watched them uncurl, turning from brown to green as they did so. Then he threw them up into the air and they fluttered away in the soft breeze. Jonny laughed.

'That's a good trick,' he said.

'I saw *you* do it,' said Dook, 'when you were making this place.'

'Back to the plan,' said Jonny, and they walked down to the beach, stood in the surf up to their knees and skimmed stones while they talked.

The next day Jonny and Dook stood outside the-door-with-no-frame. Dook had arranged to meet the girl there again. They waited. For a while nothing happened and Jonny started to worry that she may have forgotten. Then there was a click and the door swung open a little.

The girl's round, slightly freckled face peered at them through the gap. Jonny ran forward.

'Hey! it's me! Jonny! How are you?'

She seemed different. Shy. Nervous. She looked down at the ground, at Jonny's feet instead of his face. He reached out and grabbed her arm and tried to pull her through into his side, but she drew back, shaking her head. 'No. I can't come through Jonny. Not now. Not anymore. Not since we came here. Don't try and make me, something terrible will happen.'

'Says who?' asked Jonny. 'This is my world. Nothing will happen.'

She just shook her head and made a face. She was wearing a strange coat, made up of lots of patches stitched together, all different colours.

'What's the coat? asked Jonny

She brightened up. 'Do you like it? We all wear them here. Nice isn't it?'

'You all have them? Who's all of you? I thought it was just you and the boy.'

'We made lots more people Jonny. Lots of friends. Hope you don't mind.'

Jonny shook his head. Of course not. He wanted them to have friends.

'Can I come and see you all?' he asked.

'You might get into trouble,' she said.

Jonny shook his head. He didn't understand this at all. How could he get into trouble?

'I could come in disguise,' he said, 'Maybe you could get me one of those coats.'

She brightened up again. 'I could make you one. A special one. It'll only take me a day. I'll work hard. I'll work on it solidly.'

He shrugged, 'Okay, why not? See you tomorrow,' he said.

And the girl went and the door closed. Jonny reached out and touched it, but it was too hot for him.

'This is weird,' he said, 'I make a world and then I can't do what I want in it.'

Dook and Jonny stayed at the door for a while, Jonny hoping that the girl might come back, or perhaps the boy. But nothing more happened. Eventually they went off to find Firebreath Slimetongue. He was digging a huge hole in the earth.

'What's this for?' asked Jonny, putting on a cheerful smile.

Firebreath shook his head. He turned and blew out a puff of smoke towards a huge, grey, ragged mound.

'Rocktail,' said Dook, 'he's burying Rocktail.'

Firebreath finished scooping earth with his massive feet and he went to the body and began rolling it towards the hole, butting it with his forehead. Bits of grass and mud clung to the body as it rolled. It was a sad sight. Eventually the body thumped into the crater Firebreath had dug. The ground shook and Jonny trembled a little. Rocktail was too big for the hole though, and the grey body sat up out of the ground. Firebreath took a step back and Dook pulled Jonny away too.

'Stand back,' Dook said.

Firebreath let out a sound which was something like a groan and roar mixed together. A bright tear slipped from his right eye. It was patterned and coloured as if it was a reflection of the world. A second later a huge jagged burst of fire leapt from his mouth and Rocktail's body was engulfed in the lively orange flames.

Jonny and Dook stepped further back. Jonny covered his nose, expecting it to smell bad, but it didn't smell of anything. The flames quickly died down again and Rocktail's body was gone. There was just a pile of coloured ashes lining the crater. Firebreath kicked the earth back into the scorched hole and one by one other fog people stepped forward and laid new flowers on the ground. Soon the place where Rocktail was buried was a small mountain of brightly coloured petals.

Jonny sniffed and bit his lip.

'I've got to get through that door,' he said, through gritted teeth.

Dook patted his shoulder, 'You will,' he said, 'you will.'

The next day Jonny and Dook went back to the-door-with-no-frame and had to wait a long time for it to open. Eventually the girl appeared again. But she was not holding a new multi-coloured coat. Her hands were empty.

I thought you were going to make Jonny a coloured coat like yours, ' said Dook.

'He won't do it,' she said.

The girl was standing there grim faced, one foot in her world, the other through the door in Jonny's.

'He doesn't think it's a good idea at all,' she said, 'he thinks it'll just mean trouble.'

'You mean the boy?' said Jonny.

She nodded and looked down at the ground.

'I have made it,' she said quietly, 'the coat. I made you a good one, I worked all night. It looks great.'

Dook turned away from her and walked Jonny backwards a few paces.

'Let me do it,' he muttered.

'Do what?' asked Jonny.

'Go and persuade the boy,' said Dook. 'I can get in and out of there easily with the girl.'

'What about the Fog Prince?'

'He's not after me, it's you he's worried about.'

Jonny nodded and Dook went back to the-door-with-no-frame. Alone. He leant close to the girl and spoke to her softly. Jonny saw her nod and turn away. Dook followed her through the door, being careful not to touch it as he passed through the gap. Jonny looked around. Suddenly he was alone. The place was still alive with the buzzing of insects and the rustle of leaves, but there was no one around. He went for a walk. He found himself on the beach so he went swimming. It was a little colder these days and took longer for him to dry out afterwards, so he lay on the beach and dozed for a while.

'It's dark in there.'

Jonny woke and looked up. A huge figure was towering above him, all shadow against the sun. He sat up and shaded his eyes. For a moment he feared it was the Fog Prince again. It was Dook, back from the other side of the door.

'You did it?' Jonny asked.

Dook nodded. 'The boy took some persuading but I broke into one of his dreams and persuaded him. He knows what to do. He's a good lad.'

Dook flopped down beside Jonny. He blew out his cheeks and sighed. He looked tired for the first time.

'It's hard work jailbreaking into people's dreams. I could do with a nap now.'

But Jonny was on his feet. 'No time for that, we have to go with the plan now.'

Dook laughed and pulled Jonny back down.

'Patience, Jonny patience. These things take time. The girl will be back in the morning. You can go then.'

They sat and watched the sun go down. A school of dolphins emerged from the water and Jonny and Dook dived in and swam races with them. The dolphins chirruped and spun somersaults and Jonny and Dook did their best to keep up. At one point a couple of tiger sharks appeared and Jonny and Dook rode on their backs, side by side. The evening breeze ripped at their hair, and the sea sprayed up like a circle of fountains all around them. But Jonny still could not forget about the plan, he was desperate to start it as soon as possible.

'I'm not sure if I'll ever come back here again,' Jonny said as he and Dook lay collapsed on the sand afterwards.

'Why not?' said Dook.

Jonny shrugged. 'Who knows what might happen when I go through that door. And I may just wake up back home and that'll be the end of it all.'

Dook Strong shook his head. 'You won't,' he said. 'You won't wake up till everything's done.'

Jonny sat quietly for a moment, then he said, 'What's it like in there? You know – through the door?'

Dook screwed up his face. 'Dark,' he said, 'and cold. I don't like the weather much. It's nothing like this.'

'Maybe I could make it better,' said Jonny.

Dook smiled at him. His smile always reassured Jonny. 'I'm sure you can,' he said. And he reached out, tapped the sand and made a small blue plant grow up from nothing. He picked off a couple of pieces of square fruit and passed one to Jonny. It tasted like a tropical smoothie. Jonny finished it, wiped the bright blue juice from his chin, lay on his side and fell asleep.

Jonny slept for a long time and when he awoke it was the next day. They walked back to the-door-with-no-frame.

The door creaked a little as it opened. Jonny felt a draught brush his face. And there was a strange smell too. The girl appeared with a coat in her arms. She gave them a shy smile and then quickly looked down at her feet. This was the moment. Jonny turned to Dook Strong and Dook squeezed his shoulder, then gave him a hug.

'Go for it, Jonny,' Dook said quietly in his ear.

Jonny nodded, and turned back to the door.

The girl was watching them with a funny, quizzical look on her face.

Jonny took a step forward, his first step through that door with no frame. It was odd, he felt nervous, even though this was just another part of his world. The girl stepped back and let him in. Jonny glanced back for one last encouraging look to Dook, but the door was closing and he couldn't see back through there anymore.

Part Two – Beyond the Door

Chapter Fourteen

'Hey Jonny.'

The voice was familiar but it sounded a little different too.

Jonny looked past the girl. It was the boy. He wasn't smiling.

'Great to see you again,' said Jonny.

The boy nodded at him then looked away.

'Oh by the way - I'm Miriam now,' the girl said and she held out her hand as if to say, 'pleased to meet you.'

'And I'm Joey,' said the boy.

'We wanted our own names,' said the girl, as Jonny shook her hand a little awkwardly.

'Did you pick them?' Jonny asked.

They looked at one another for a moment then the girl shook her head.

'The king gave them to us,' she said.

'The king?'

Jonny looked around. They were alone, just the three of them. He took his first look at the place. There was very little grass, just a few patches here and there. The ground was mostly dark earth and pools of muddy water. There were a few straggly trees in the distance. And beyond them a line of shadowy buildings and shacks. A weak sun glinted and winked at them above the craggy stonework. Jonny shivered again.

'You cold?' Miriam asked him and she held out the coat. 'It's warm,' she said.

Jonny took it and held it up. It was all colours stitched together. There was a thick fleece lining on the inside. It would have been way too hot to wear on the other side of the door, but not here. Here Jonny needed the warmth, he pulled it on.

So where did you get them then?' he asked.

'What?' asked Joey. 'The coats? We make 'em. Or swap things for them.'

'The names,' said Jonny. 'Where did you get the names?'

'The king,' said Miriam, 'he gives everybody names.'

'I didn't know you had a king,' said Jonny.

Miriam's face lit up. 'Yes you did. You know him.'

Jonny felt a strange feeling in his stomach. Joey pulled out a black leather wallet and pulled out a piece of grey paper.

'That's him,' he said. 'He's on all our money.'

Jonny took the note and the feeling in his stomach grew worse. On the front of the note was a picture of the Fog Prince.

'But he's not a *king*,' said Jonny, 'he's the...'

Miriam clapped a hand over Jonny's mouth. Her eyes flashed wide and she shook her head. Just once, but very firmly.

'We don't talk about that,' she said quietly.

'Wanna meet some of the others,' said Joey, interrupting quickly.

Jonny nodded. 'Do they know I'm coming?'

Joey laughed. 'Hardly. You're not big round here Jonny. No one knows about you. We don't talk about it much really.'

They began to walk, Jonny had to work hard to sidestep the muddy puddles. Bits of litter blew past them as they went.

'What do you mean? You don't talk about it much?' he asked.

'You know, the old days,' said Joey. 'When we did stuff with you. Our friends aren't interested. They have other things to worry about.'

Jonny glanced at Miriam, she was looking at him sideways, biting her lip and looking nervous. She raised a finger and jabbed ahead.

'That's where we hang out,' she said.

Jonny stopped and stared. In front of them there was a piece of grey ground surrounded by a low crumbling stone wall. A couple of iron gates hung off dirty cracked gateposts. The ground inside was full of large bits of stone sticking out of the earth.

'We have picnics here,' said Miriam. She patted her cloth shoulder bag, it was made of the same coloured patches. 'I bought some food we can have now.'

'There's Dig and Rooster,' said Joey and he hurried on ahead.

He jumped the wall and ran over to a couple of others who were huddling near a smoking fire. Jonny and Miriam followed him. Jonny clambered over the wall then stopped to study one of the bits of stone. It said *Keggle, 12*.

'What's this' Jonny asked.

'Oh that's Keggle's grave, Jonny. Lots of our friends are here.'

'Already? But you haven't been here that long.'

Miriam shrugged. 'Seems like we've been here ages.' she said.

She held out a thick, white packet. 'Want some unicorn, cabbage and maggot pie?'

'Unicorn? Really?' said Jonny, and then he thought and looked about. 'That reminds me.

Can I see Shimmersteel? I haven't seen him lately. I heard he came here.'

Miriam looked embarrassed now. Her face changed colour a bit and she chewed her lip again.

'Shimmersteel's dead, Jonny,' she said quietly. 'They're all dead.'

'All?' said Jonny.

'We made lots more unicorns,' she said, 'we thought they were great. Different coloured horns and hooves and everything. But I think we made them too well.'

'Why?'

'Some of our friends got the idea they'd like to use bits of the unicorns to decorate their houses and wear round their necks. So the big hunt started.'

'The big hunt?'

Miriam waved towards the others, she started walking again, unwrapping the pie as she went. Jonny followed her. Dig and Rooster barely looked at Jonny as he said hello to them.

They all sat down amongst the broken bits of stone. There were jagged shards of broken glass, twisted bits of litter and some rusted cans among the rocks. Miriam handed round the bits of pie.

'I was telling our friend Jonny about the big hunt,' she said.

Rooster snorted and laughed, spitting bits of pie as he did it.

'That was stupid,' he said.

'What happened? Jonny asked.

'They killed 'em all,' said Rooster, 'every last unicorn that ever was, just so they can stick bits of them on their gateposts.'

'Rooster made the best unicorn. It was byootiful,' said Dig.

Joey nodded. 'It was,' he said and he bit into his pie and scowled.

Jonny tried a bit, it tasted like cardboard and damp sponge.

Miriam shrugged. 'Sorry. The pie's not great is it?'

'It's all we got,' said Rooster,

'You don't usually complain,' said Joey.

'Sorry,' mumbled Miriam.

Chapter Fifteen

Jonny looked about, he found one of the smoother stones and took it in his hands. He closed his eyes and held it for a while.

'What you doing?' said Dig.

Jonny opened his eyes and held out his hands. Miriam sniffed. There was the smell of new bread. Jonny was holding a warm, freshly baked loaf. Miriam's eyes popped wide. Dig snorted. Jonny broke the bread and passed pieces of it round. It tasted good. Very good.

'Do that again,' said Dig.

Jonny thought for a moment then shook his head.

'One's enough,' he said.

'I don't care - do it again,' Dig snarled. His eyes flashed red. He was a big lad, with scars on his face and knuckles. His skin was rough and red, as if he'd spent too much time out in the cold.

'No, I made this bread 'cause we're hungry, and it's good food. This bread will feed you well. But you don't need another. It's not magic.'

'Don't waste your time,' said Rooster, 'it's just a trick, all those kinds of things are tricks. You can't make bread from stones. It's just not logical.'

Rooster was much smaller than Dig. Jonny couldn't quite see his eyes as he had a long fringe which fell down and covered them.

'But we do things like this all the time where I come from,' said Jonny.

'Then do it again now,' said Dig.

'We don't do it to impress people,' said Jonny. 'It's not about that. It's just life.'

Dig began clenching and unclenching his big fists.

'You're a big fat fake,' he said.

'He's a con artist,' said Rooster. 'I've heard about them. They go about doing tricks and pretending they're some kind of hero.'

'He's not a hero - look at him,' said Dig. 'He's weedy and scrawny. Like you Rooster. All brains and no brawn.'

Joey laughed, but then he moved himself back a little from Dig.

'At least I got a brain,' said Rooster, and for a moment he pushed his fringe away. His eyes were small and narrow, he had dark circles under them.

'Shuttup, Roosty,' said Dig.

'You shut up, Digsy,' said Rooster.

'No, you shuttup.'

'No, you.'

Dig turned on Rooster and he threw himself at the other boy. They rolled over and over, smashing into gravestones and muddy puddles.

Miriam gave Jonny a quick smile, her lips pressed tightly together.

'It's a bit different here, isn't it?' she said.

Jonny nodded. 'Has it always been like this?' he asked.

'Not at first,' she said, 'at first it was a lot like your world, and we had fun making lots of new things. But somehow it got out of hand, and we made new friends and they made new friends and people started breaking things.'

'Don't tell him all that,' said Joey.

'Why not?' asked Miriam.

Joey stood up and threw his bread into a puddle. 'Because it's none of his business.'

Dig and Rooster were still wrestling as Joey turned and walked away.

'He's sad about Keggle,' said Miriam. 'He was his best friend.'

Jonny glanced over towards the nearby gravestone, the one with Keggle's name on it.

'He wasn't my best friend,' Joey snapped as he swung round to look back at her.

'Well you were always together,' she said.

Jonny stood up and walked to the grave.

'I think I can do something about this,' he said, and he knelt down, his knees in the claggy, wet mud.

He knelt quietly for a moment then suddenly began shoving his hands into the grave scooping out the dirt.

'No!' yelled Joey, so loud that Dig and Rooster stopped their fighting to see what was going on. 'Get out of there!' Joey yelled.

But it was too late, Jonny had already dug deep enough for a pale dead hand to appear sticking out of the grave.

The dead, white hand stuck out of the earth as if it was waving for help. But it wasn't, it wasn't moving and it wasn't alive. Miriam gasped, Joey was angry, Dig and Rooster stopped their fighting and came closer.

'You'd better hurry up and bury that again,' said Dig, 'the king doesn't like things looking untidy round here.'

Jonny couldn't help but smile.

'Untidy?' he said, looking around at the broken glass and dirty litter everywhere.

Jonny reached out towards the hand.

'Don't,' said Joey.

'No, let him,' said Miriam.

'Is this more magic?' said Dig.

'Another con trick you mean,' said Rooster.

Jonny ignored them all. He pushed his hand towards the fingers of the cold, white hand. The moment his fingers made contact the dead fingers shuddered and flicked, like they'd had an electric shock. Jonny reached out and grabbed the hand, the hand responded and the cold, white fingers wrapped around his. Suddenly there was the sound of a cough.

'Don't do that,' said Dig, 'you made me jump.'

'Wasn't me,' said Rooster.

'It... it... it came from the grave,' said Miriam. 'It must have been Keggle.'

'Keggle!?' said Dig.

Jonny stood up and pulled with all his might. The earth began to open up and a muddy arm then a head poked out. Jonny pulled again and Miriam came to help. Together they hauled the boy out of the ground and let him fall with a slap beside his own grave. The body coughed and spluttered and gasped for air. Miriam leant over the face and scooped the earth from the eyes. Keggle blinked and spat a mouthful of soil into the air. Then he sat up, looked around and smiled. There were bits of mud between his teeth. He looked very happy though. He pulled a worm from behind his ear, put it down and let it crawl away.

'Hello,' he said.

And Rooster fainted.

'Wow!' said Dig.

'Wow indeed,' said a cold, sly voice.

Suddenly a smoggy cloud fell over the graveyard and one by one dark figures stepped out of the shadows. Jonny turned and heard that cold, sly voice again. It was the Fog Prince.

'Didn't think we'd ever see you here,' he was saying. 'You're a long way from home.' He was wearing a long purple leather coat, splashed with mud around the bottom. His purple boots were dirty too. His face was as cloudy as ever, a swirling mass of fog and anger.

Chapter Sixteen

'What have you done to my world?' Jonny said, his eyes blazing at the prince.

'It's my world now,' sneered the prince. 'You lost it. And you lost all these too. They're not with you anymore.'

Jonny looked around, Miriam, Joey and Dig were kneeling down in the mud, their heads bowed. Rooster was lying on his back, out cold. Keggle was still sitting there, breathing new air and looking around blinking. Miriam kept glancing up at Jonny.

'Nothing to say for yourself?' sneered the Fog Prince.

'I need to help Keggle,' said Jonny and he reached down and offered the boy his hand.

'You shouldn't be meddling here Jonny, you don't belong,' said the Fog Prince.

'This is all my world, prince,' Jonny said as he pulled Keggle up.

The Fog Prince snarled. 'I made this!' he snapped, 'and I'm king of it now. King! You got it? KING!'

He stepped over to Jonny and grabbed his face by the chin. He forced Jonny to look right at him.

'And the problem for you,' sneered the prince, 'is this - you don't have all your foggy friends here to look after you. Especially not that dumb Dook.'

The Fog Prince laughed and his breath smelt bad. Like a strange mixture of rotten eggs, damp dogs and petrol. He spat and his spit was a fiery yellow colour. 'You're in trouble Jonny, your little rescue plan is over before it's even begun.' He snapped his long jagged fingers. 'Get him!'

The Fog Prince's men let out a blood curdling shriek and came lurching for Jonny, arms outstretched like an army of zombies. Jonny leapt backwards, nearly tripping over Rooster on the ground. Jonny reached down, picked up the sleeping boy and threw him over his shoulder.

'Follow me!' he yelled to the others and with a sudden burst of energy he turned and ran through the graveyard. Miriam, Dig and Joey jumped up and followed, the prince's men only seconds behind them. Jonny was up ahead leaping grave stones and searching for a way out. Rooster bounced up and down on his shoulder as he went. He was still out cold. Rooster wasn't light but Jonny felt much stronger than he normally did. But then there was another shriek from the prince's army and Jonny felt himself suddenly growing tired.

The Fog Prince's men were closing on them. Jonny could hear them puffing and panting as they tripped over the grave stones, and they were definitely getting louder. They were hissing and spitting threats as they came, bragging about the terrible things they were going to do to Jonny and the others when they caught them. Keggle overtook Jonny and ran ahead of him, he may have only just come back from the dead, but that boy could run. Dig was slower, struggling to keep up and Jonny couldn't see Miriam or Joey at all. Suddenly they ran into a grey smoggy cloud. It seemed to drop on them in an instant. Then Jonny heard Miriam's voice.

'Quick! In here.'

He felt a hand grab his shoulder and steer him to the right. He trusted it and followed, grabbing at Keggle and pulling him in too as he went. Jonny's feet hit uneven rocks and he tripped and fell. Rooster made an 'Oof!' sound as he fell off Jonny's shoulders. They crouched in the damp darkness for a while. Other bodies came stumbling past Jonny, but he didn't move. Then he heard the sound of the Fog Prince's army passing by, and he smelt the stench of them too. Their threats thundered around as they yelped at one another in the smog. Jonny sat tight and didn't move, hoping that all the others had followed Miriam off the path.

After a while the hissing voices faded and the pounding feet slapped into the distance. And then the smog lifted. Jonny looked around. They were sitting in a cave. Keggle was blinking and rubbing his arms and legs, as if he was massaging some life back into them. Rooster was rubbing his head. It may well have got bruises when he fell from Jonny's shoulder. Miriam gave Jonny a big smile. Joey and Dig sat hunched, backs against the cave wall, hugging their legs to their chests. They scowled and said nothing.

'That was close,' said Keggle, with a grin.

'I'm Jonny,' said Jonny and he held out his hand towards Keggle.

Keggle took it and shook it enthusiastically, he still had soil and grass all over his hand, but it wasn't dead white any more. It was pink and alive.

'Well done Miriam,' said Jonny.

'I remembered this cave was here,' she said.

Jonny looked around and nodded.

'I wonder why the prince was so mad with me?' Jonny said.

'It's obvious,' said Joey, 'because of Keggle.'

'Keggle? Why?'

But Joey just shrugged and said nothing more.

Dig stood up. 'I'm hungry,' he said and he waved his big scarred hand towards the mouth of the cave. 'Let's get some grub.'

'Is it safe?' asked Rooster.

But Dig didn't reply, he just lumbered past them to the entrance and looked out. Jonny followed him and was suddenly aware of the sound of the sea. They had left the graveyard behind and were on a beach. The sand stretched for miles, but it was grey and spattered with bits of litter, not clean and golden. There was no sign of the Fog Prince or his army. A shape leapt up out of the surf.

'A shark!' said Jonny, 'Did you see that! A shark. Let's go swimming!'

Joey laughed and stepped up beside him.

'I don't think so,' he muttered, 'you can't swim with sharks round here Jonny. They'll eat you.'

'Eat me? Really? Why?' Jonny was amazed.

Joey shrugged. 'Just the way it is. Oh and be careful with what you go eating too. You can't just grab any old thing. Stuff is poisonous.'

Jonny crouched and pulled some bright turquoise seaweed off a rock.

'Yea, like that,' said Joey and he grabbed it off Jonny and flung it away. 'Might look pretty but it'll give you the kind of stomach ache you never get over.'

Dig was tramping up the beach towards the sea. 'Come on,' he yelled, 'we got some fish to catch.'

Joey waved towards Dig. 'He'll get us some good food,' he said.

Dig waded out into the shallows and stood there for a while, waiting. The others gathered on the beach, watching Dig and the shark in the distance. The shark leapt in and out of the waves but it didn't come close to Dig. Miriam kept glancing up and down the beach.

'What's wrong with you?' asked Joey.

'Just checking for the king's men,' she said.

Rooster looked startled. 'Where?' he asked.

'In your brain,' said Joey tapping his skull. 'They've gone.'

Suddenly there was a shout from the sea. They looked and saw Dig holding up a large fish in both hands. He had a big triumphant grin on his face, then he looked disappointed.

'Where's the fire?' he called. 'We gotta cook this monster.'

Jonny and the others ran about grabbing bits of damp driftwood.

'This'll never burn,' said Rooster, but they kept piling it up.

Eventually, when they had a good sized woodpile Jonny crouched down beside it.

He narrowed his eyes, looked up at the sky then looked back down at the wood. There was a sudden gust of wind and a spark landed on the wood and a flame flared. Before long the fire was blazing.

Dig brought the prize catch and they made space amongst the flames to cook it. When it was ready they tucked in. It was delicious.

'Let's tidy the beach,' said Jonny when they'd finished eating.

The others looked horrified.

'Don't be illogical, it's massive,' said Rooster.

'We can make a start,' said Jonny.

'D'you think it's really worth it?' said Miriam.

Jonny stood up, licking bits of fish from his fingers. 'Let's find out,' he said.

Chapter Seventeen

Jonny began walking along the grey, muck-strewn sand. He found an old orange sack under a piece of driftwood and began putting the bits of dirty litter into it.

'Why don't you just do one of your magic tricks and get the beach to clean itself up,' called Rooster.

Jonny turned and grinned at him. 'It doesn't work like that,' he said, and he walked on.

He heard footsteps nearby and glanced sideways to see Miriam collecting a few old tins, she slipped them into the sack with a shy smile.

Jonny stopped and pointed up ahead.

'What's that?' he said.

'Looks like a bundle of old rags,' said Miriam. 'They often get washed up round here.'

Jonny walked closer. It did look exactly like a bundle of old rags, just piled up high there on the sand. He ran ahead, put down the orange sack and crouched down beside it. And that's when the bundle coughed.

Jonny jumped, Miriam came over.

The bundle shuddered and lifted up its old pale head. It wasn't just a pile of rags, there was a woman in there. Her skin was thin and very white. Her eyes were a strange milky colour.

'It's one of the mad mist people,' said Miriam.

'The mad mist people?'

'Yes,' said Miriam, 'the king sometimes puts a spell on people he doesn't like. They end up like this. Just hanging around. Staring. Wearing old rags. Going nowhere. It's spooky.'

'Careful, those mad misters bite.' It was Dig, he came bounding up to see what was going on. He had bits of fish caked around his mouth.

'They don't bite,' said Joey, coming up behind him. 'That's just what people say.'

'Are there many mad mist people?' asked Jonny.

'More every day,' said Joey.

Jonny placed a hand on the woman's raggedy shoulder. She turned and looked at him, but her eyes had that strange milky stare. Jonny stood up and walked a few steps away. He looked at her carefully then came back again. He reached down and scooped up a handful of grey sand, held it to his mouth and breathed on it a couple of times. By now Rooster had arrived and he was tapping his temple as if to say, 'Jonny's mad.'

Jonny took the scoop of sand and split it in two, a finger-full in each hand. Then he carefully pressed the two small piles against the woman's eyes.

'Yow!' said Rooster, 'that's gonna sting.'

'Shuttup, Roosty,' said Dig.

'You shuttup, Digsy,' said Rooster.

The larger boy turned and threw himself at the other boy and they went tumbling on the sand. No one paid much attention, all eyes were on Jonny as he took the woman's hands and encouraged her to smear the damp sand from her eyes. For a moment she sat there with her fingers pressed on her face doing nothing, and Jonny feared she might just stay that way. Then suddenly her fingers tensed and flicked and she started scraping the sand from her right eye. She blinked twice and scraped again, then she scooped the sand from her left eye too. She stopped and sat suddenly still, and for the longest time nothing happened. Then she turned her head sharply and gasped at Jonny. Her eyes were clear and a warm, bright, brown colour. She clamped a sandy hand to her mouth and then let out a laugh.

Dig and Rooster stopped their wrestling and looked over. The bundle of rags was standing up and making a lot of noise. She was spinning around unsteadily, blinking furiously and pressing her hands on and off her face. Miriam and Joey were watching wide-eyed. Keggle was laughing and clapping his hands.

Miriam grabbed Jonny's shoulder. 'You're going to do it, aren't you?' she said. 'I told Keggle you were going to do it.'

'Do what?' said Jonny. He was busy watching the woman as she leapt up and wandered off across the beach, stopping every so often to pick up shells and study them intently.

'You're going to make this place better. You're gonna fix it, aren't you? So it's just like your world.'

Jonny stood up and looked at Miriam, then at the others. For some reason everyone had stopped and was staring at him.

'When did you tell Keggle?' he asked.

'What?' she said.

'When did you tell Keggle I was going to change things?'

Miriam's smile faded. 'You know before the... before he...'

'Before the Fog Prince killed him,' said Jonny. 'That's what happened, isn't it? You told Keggle I was coming and he told everyone else. And that's when the Fog Prince killed him.'

Keggle looked confused. 'I thought it was good news,' he said. 'You're going to make everything better.'

'It is good news,' said Jonny. 'But not everyone will think so. You know what the Fog Prince is like.'

'But he can't hurt you, Jonny,' said Joey. 'Can he?'

Jonny looked at them and shrugged his shoulders. But he didn't say yes or no.

'She didn't tell Keggle,' said Joey, chasing after Jonny as he continued picking up rubbish from the beach.

Jonny turned to look at him.

'What do you mean?'

'We didn't tell Keggle. That isn't why the king wanted to kill Keggle. And anyway Keggle was already sick...'

Jonny looked at Joey.

'Remember the good times we had Joey,' he said. 'Remember everything we made together?'

The boy lowered his eyes and looked at the sand.

'Things are different now,' Joey said. 'We got tricked.'

'Things *are* different Joey. For one thing you never told lies to me before.'

'Lies?'

'The king – as you call him – will do anything to ruin things, Joey. Don't help him by lying. Remember - he's the real liar, not you. He's not even a king. He's the Fog Prince. He did kill Keggle for talking about me, didn't he?'

Joey kept looking down at the sand. Then he shrugged and looked up again. 'Can you make it all better?' he asked.

'Not the way you think,' said Jonny. 'But I have a plan.'

He turned and walked on and kept on collecting bits of rubbish. Joey bent down and grabbed at a rusty can. He recoiled and jammed his thumb into his mouth.

'Ow!' he yelped.

Jonny walked back to him and pulled the thumb from his mouth.

'That rusty old can cut me,' said Joey.

Jonny nodded. 'You have to be careful doing this stuff.'

He turned and walked on again.

'Hey!' said Joey. 'Aren't you going to make it better?'

'Doesn't work like that,' said Jonny. He stopped, thought for a moment then turned back, reached into his pocket and held out a small brown band-aid. He peeled off the white strips and pressed it round Joey's injured thumb and walked away.

'I don't understand you,' said Joey.

'Of course not,' Jonny called back, 'because you're you and I'm me.'

Chapter Eighteen

Jonny kept on picking up bits of rubbish, but his feet were feeling heavy now and his body was tired. The others helped out, but they were happy when they stopped at another cave and built a fire. Dig went fishing again but couldn't find any big fish. Jonny had a look at the sea and pointed.

'Over there,' he called to Dig.

'How d'you know?'

'Try it,' said Jonny.

Dig shook his head. 'There won't be any over there.'

'Try it,' said Jonny, but Dig shook his head and stayed where he was.

After a while Dig came up the beach with something in his hand. It was the smallest fish in the world.

'That won't feed us,' said Joey.

'Well you try then, genius,' said Dig.

'I told you' said Jonny, 'try over there.'

Jonny stood up and walked back towards the sea. No one followed. At first. Then slowly, one by one, they walked down to the water's edge. Jonny pointed again. Dig huffed and sighed and shook his head, but he waded into the sea, watched for a moment then shoved his hands under the water. He yelped and came up holding two very large fish.

Dig came bounding out of the sea, spraying them all with water.

Rooster nodded and flicked back the fringe from his eyes. 'Clever,' he said. 'Very clever.'

Keggle grabbed the fish and ran back up the beach to start cooking. They all tucked in and the meal was delicious, but Joey and Miriam said very little, and Rooster was trying hard to work out how Jonny had done it. Only Keggle chatted happily with Jonny.

Jonny wasn't enjoying his dream any more. It had been okay at the start, making new friends and creating lots of things, but now it felt different and he didn't like it. He wanted to wake up. But he couldn't. Sometimes in the past he'd been able to break out of bad dreams and go down to the kitchen for a glass of milk and a biscuit. He wanted to do that now but he couldn't and it was beginning to feel a bit like a nightmare.

'I need a walk,' said Jonny, 'anyone coming?'

It was growing dark and they were all huddled around the fire, clutching their coats around them for warmth. Joey and Miriam shook their head. Keggle leapt up.

'I'll come,' he said, 'and you Dig, you'll come, won't you?'

Dig shrugged.

'What about me?' said Rooster.

'Up to you,' said Jonny quietly, and he started walking.

When he glanced back a few minutes later Keggle and Dig were wandering along behind him. But there was no sign of Rooster.

'Where are we going?' asked Keggle.

'You'll see,' said Jonny.

Then he stopped and looked at the other two. 'What did you hear about me, Keggle?'

'What?' Keggle looked a little bewildered.

'From Miriam, what did she tell you? Before I got here.'

Keggle scratched his head for a moment then grinned. 'She told me that you could sort things out.'

Jonny nodded. 'And did she say why?'

Keggle thought for a moment. 'Something about you understanding how things all fitted together. Yea, that's right. Cause you made everything here. At the start. Yea, that's what she said.'

'And what do you think now?'

'Now?' Keggle shrugged. 'What can I say? The king nuked me and yet here I am still breathing. You sorted that out.'

'What about you, Dig?'

'What about me what?'

'What do you think?' said Jonny.

'I think you should nuke the king. And I reckon you could easily do it.'

Jonny laughed. 'Come on,' he said, 'we got lots of things to do and none of them involves nuking anybody.'

Chapter Nineteen

They met others on the beach as they walked and each time Jonny stopped to talk to them. Sometimes they met a group, sometimes people on their own. One or two mad misters. One man sat shivering in the semi-darkness, knees pulled close to his chest. But he was no mad mister, there was no spell on him, he just had no coloured coat. Jonny peeled off his, the one Miriam had made for him, and he handed it to the man who gratefully pulled it around his shoulders.

'Miriam won't be happy you gave that away,' said Dig as they walked on, 'she worked through the night to make it for you.'

Jonny said nothing, he just pointed out to where the silver, moonlit sea was breaking on the sand. There was a small brown boat tied to a stake in the sand. He started walking towards it.

'That'll never float,' said Dig.

'Let's find out,' said Jonny.

He untied it and began to push it towards the water, Keggle helped him. Dig just watched. The waves lifted it off the ground and they jumped in.

Jonny looked back towards Dig.

'Last call for the boat trip,' he said.

Dig frowned. 'I'm not going out there, it's full of storms and monsters.'

'Well then - last call for the boat trip to the storms and monsters,' said Jonny.

He and Keggle picked up the old oars and pushed them into the water. The boat was drifting further out, Dig was going to have to get wet if he was going to climb in now. He huffed and sighed and shook his head.

'That's not how you work those oars,' he growled. 'Ohhh, I must be mad,' and he sloshed through the water towards them and climbed in.

The oars were rotting and splintered but Dig was good at rowing and he and Keggle made the best of moving the boat out to sea.

'Where are we going?' Dig muttered.

'Forward,' said Jonny, and he curled up in the back and closed his eyes.

The sea exploded. It was as if someone had set off a huge bomb under the surface. A massive head of water burst out and upward, showering the boat with saturating spray. Dig and Keggle had to wipe their eyes to see anything. Suddenly a second head burst from the waves, but this one was lime green and had fiery eyes. It threw back its head and roared, and the sound made the boat shudder.

'This is it,' said Dig. 'I warned you. This is the end.'

But no one was listening. Keggle was frantically trying to row them away from the monster, and Jonny was fast asleep in the back. Dig just stared as the creature rose higher and higher out of the water.

'We're going to die,' he said.

The monster turned on them and smashed his head onto the surface of the sea. The tidal wave that followed lifted the boat high up into the air. It shot up so fast that it flew off the water and hovered in mid-air for a moment. This was just as well because the monster opened its jaws to bite the boat and crack it in two, but the boat wasn't there. It was still hovering above him and the creature could only bite on thin air. Dig and Keggle clung on to the sides and yelled. Jonny rolled over and blinked at them.

'Everything all right?' he asked.

There was a massive crack as thunder shook the sky and lightning streaked across the horizon.

'No everything's not all right!' shouted Dig.

Keggle tried to smile but he was hanging on to the side with all his might.

Jonny leant over and looked down.

'How did we get up here?' he asked.

'That!' said Dig and he pointed at the monster's lime green snout as the boat began to fall past it back to the sea.

'Oh I see,' said Jonny. 'Don't...' And he said something else but it was drowned out by another huge clap of thunder.

'Don't what?' called Keggle.

'I said...' another clap of thunder drowned out his words.

Jonny waited for it to subside.

'I said, don't worry it'll be all right,' said Jonny and as he spoke the boat slammed back into the water and a wall of spray flew up all around them.

'All right? All right? You're kidding aren't you? If that monster doesn't get us then the storm will,' shouted Dig.

Jonny looked up. The creature was looming right over the boat, its jaws open wide, its teeth jagged and dripping with dark green spit. Dig shielded his head, Keggle waved an oar at the sea monster. Then the boat lurched in the water and a second head appeared. A giant inky blue octopus, with eyes like saucers, rose out of the water on the other side of the boat. They were surrounded.

The octopus glanced at the green monster for a moment as if waiting for a signal. The monster glared back at the octopus.

Keggle hurled his oar at the lime green monster and smacked it on the nose. The monster gave an ear splitting roar. The inky blue octopus sucked its octopus cheeks in and spat out a spray of blue sticky slime. Keggle ducked and the gloop smacked Dig right in the face. The octopus then raised a huge tentacle, it was as thick as a tree trunk and lined with deadly suckers. The creature swung it in an arc towards Keggle, who dodged again so that the tentacle struck Dig and scooped him right off the boat. The octopus hurled him up into the air and juggled him from one tentacle to another. Dig yelled as he spun upside-down and he clapped his hands over his mouth to stop himself being sick. The octopus held Dig by the leg and dangled him over the green monster's open mouth.

'QUIET!' yelled Jonny and his voice boomed as if he was speaking into a microphone.

In the dark sky above them thunder crashed and lightning followed it.

'I said - QUIET!' yelled Jonny again as he stood up, and everything fell suddenly still. The storm and the action both stopped as if someone had pressed a giant pause button.

The monster and the octopus stared at Jonny as if they'd only just seen him there. The sea dropped into an unnatural calm. The thunder faded and there was no more lightning cutting jagged lines across the sky.

'Enough now,' said Jonny, quietly. 'It's over.'

The green monster opened its mouth a little wider to swallow Dig but Jonny raised a hand.

'Enough,' he said, and he lay back down in the boat and closed his eyes.

The monster sighed, the octopus shrugged and began to lower Dig back into the boat. At the last moment the octopus let go and Dig fell in an untidy heap. Then both creatures sank back into the sea, the monster rumbling as it went. The water lapped quietly against the boat. Keggle and Dig looked at one another. Dig opened his mouth to say something when there were was a distant explosion and something red and glowing fell out of the sky and went sizzling past them into the sea.

'What was that?' asked Keggle.

'A lava ball from the volcano on Mount Rumble. The place where we're going. Keep rowing guys,' said Jonny, from where he was lying in the back of the boat with his eyes still shut.

'We're going to Mount Rumble?' said Dig.

Jonny nodded.

'We'll die,' said Dig.
Jonny shrugged.

Chapter Twenty

Dig and Keggle just looked at each other. Keggle's face was white and Dig still had octopus ink splodged all over him. They said nothing more, they just went back to rowing, but they were thinking a lot. They'd seen nothing like this before. The sea was full of dangers and monsters and the best thing to do was to avoid them all, not face them head on like this. They rowed on as more lava balls spun through the sky and spattered in the water round the boat. Dig and Keggle flinched and ducked each time, Jonny continued his dozing. Before long a dark triangular shadow rose up on the horizon. Smoke and flame spurted from the top.

'Mount Rumble,' Dig muttered. Jonny sat up and rubbed his eyes. He looked over the side of the boat. The sea was a lot calmer but still choppy here and there. But to Jonny it looked suddenly quite solid. He stood up, put his hand on the side of the boat and threw one foot out and onto the water.

'What are you doing?' yelled Dig.

Jonny looked back and smiled and climbed right out.

Jonny's feet connected with the water. The sea felt wet and cold and uneven. Jonny glanced up at Mount Rumble, it was a way off yet but he reckoned he could make it. He forgot about the sea and kept walking. Behind him voices were calling out. He glanced back. Dig was staring with his mouth wide open. He had blue splodges on his cheeks. Keggle was laughing and pointing in amazement. Jonny waved towards them.

'Have you ever been to Mount Rumble?' he asked.

Keggle shook his head.

'This is your chance to walk it,' said Jonny.

Dig looked at Jonny then down at the water.

'Are you serious?' said Dig.

'Don't worry,' said Jonny. 'Just try.'

Dig looked down again, then at Keggle.

'Don't tell the others I tried this okay?' Dig said. 'You got me?'

Keggle grinned and nodded. He watched as Dig threw his leg over the side.

Dig could feel his heart pumping in his chest. Jonny was walking further away on the waves. It was now or never.

'I must be mad,' he muttered, but he did it anyway.

He jabbed his other foot out of the boat and onto the sea and then he straightened up.

'I can do it!' he yelled. 'I can do it!'

And he threw back his head and whooped into the night sky. He took a few blundering steps and moved towards Jonny. Jonny looked back and nodded. Dig glanced back at Keggle, Keggle grinned at him, but he shook his head when Dig waved to him to come too.

'Too scary,' he called out. 'Too deep.'

Dig looked down at the water. Keggle's words rang in his head. Too scary. Too deep. They got louder. Too scary. Too deep. They grew so loud that he couldn't hear Jonny calling to him.

'Come on,' said Jonny, 'let's try running to Mount Rumble.'

Too scary. Too deep. It was all Dig could hear. He'd taken four steps somehow, but his mind did not believe it. Sooner or later he wouldn't be able to keep walking and then he'd fall and drown.

It was sooner rather than later. Even as he thought about sinking his feet began to slip beneath the water. It was as if someone had sliced two holes in the ground beneath him. He could feel himself falling.

'Agh! Help!!' he yelled.

He looked back at Keggle. His smile had turned to horror. Keggle reached out a hand to grab Dig but Dig had moved too far from the boat. Dig was sinking too fast and the water was deathly cold. It was all over. He could see himself slipping beneath the waves, not being able to breathe any more. He had been right. The sea was going to kill him. He shut his eyes and felt himself start to die.

Chapter Twenty One

'Hey! Relax!'

Dig could hear a voice in the distance. Maybe this was heaven and maybe it was God speaking to him. He opened his eyes. He was lying in the boat. He was very wet.

Jonny and Keggle were looking down on him.

'Wh... wh... what... happened?' he said, and as he spoke he spat out a mouthful of water.

'You sank,' said Keggle.

'You walked on water,' said Jonny. 'We both did.'

'But... how did I get here?' Dig asked.

'Jonny reached out and grabbed you from under the water. He pulled you out and shoved you back in the boat. I thought you were dead!'

'I thought I was dead!' spluttered Dig, still spitting sea water from his mouth.

'You just passed out,' said Jonny.

'You looked pretty scared out there,' said Keggle.

Dig sat up and shook his head, water sprayed from his hair and ears.

'I didn't, I don't do that sort of thing. I don't get scared,' he snarled.

Keggle laughed. 'Okay then' he said, 'you looked terrified then!'

Dig shook his head again. 'No way. Not me. I'm no coward.'

'You will be soon,' said Jonny.

'No I won't!' yelled Dig.

But Jonny nodded. 'Soon. But you'll get over it. And when you do, you'll be different and you'll be able to help Keggle and the others.' Jonny jabbed his thumb towards Keggle. 'He didn't even risk getting out of the boat remember.'

But Dig just shook his head. 'I don't get scared,' he muttered.

Jonny turned and pointed and at the same time the boat jolted.

Keggle fell backwards.

'What was that?' asked Dig, grabbing the side for support.

'Mount Rumble,' said Jonny. 'We're here.'

They looked up. The boat had snagged on a couple of spiky, grey rocks. Above them the smoking mountain loomed large. There was the smell of smoke and sulphur in the air.

'Please tell me we're not going up there,' said Dig.

Jonny didn't tell him that, he just helped Keggle up and out of the boat and together they dragged the vessel out of the sea onto some shiny black sand. Behind him Mount Rumble coughed and spluttered and spat another glowing lava ball into the air. Dig looked as if he might pass out again, even though he absolutely and totally never got scared.

As Jonny walked across the shiny black sand towards Mount Rumble he started to feel sad and gloomy again. For a while things had been exciting - fighting the monsters at sea and walking on the water. And for some reason Jonny had not felt scared by any of it. Maybe he hadn't been worried because he knew it was all a dream, and in dreams you think differently. He also knew where he was taking Dig and Keggle, though he'd never been there before. The idea had popped into his mind as if it had been there all along, waiting in the shadows to jump out and surprise him. He was hoping it would lift him out of the sadness he had felt at seeing their land. It was so different here on this side of the door. Like the world he had made - yet not. It was like a messed up, grey, unfriendly version of things. And now he felt suddenly sad and just wanted to wake up again. But he couldn't.

His heart lurched a bit and his stomach flipped over inside as he looked towards Mount Rumble. He knew they had to climb it and reach the top, but suddenly it felt like a difficult thing to do. Lumps of molten lava continued to fly past them and hiss loudly as they landed in the sea. Sparks showered and smoke was in the air all around them. It smelt very bad. So why was he going? Why was he risking taking Dig and Keggle up there? He thought it was a good idea, all part of his plan, but he had some doubts too. The best thing was to just start walking. Sometimes a tough journey like this is worth it. That's what Jonny told himself as he started climbing. As he went he thought about his life back home. He'd often daydreamed about being a superhero when he'd been bored in school. Just like in those comics he read. Spiderman, Superman, Batman. Never thought it would ever turn out like this though. Never really believed he'd find himself in this kind of story. This dream was turning out like a comic book adventure. Fighting bad guys and monsters, scaling mountains and doing other incredible things. If only his school friends could see him now. They'd never believe it. Normally Jonny was no big hero. He actually liked a quiet life.

It was hot on Mount Rumble but Dig was happy about that. His clothes were still wet and clambering up the volcano was helping to dry them out. Every so often the side of the mountain rattled and rumbled, and Dig was not so happy about that. Neither was Keggle. Keggle had a vivid imagination and he could see streams of red hot lava running down the mountain at them, melting their feet, turning them to toast and sweeping them back into the sea. But it wasn't really happening, it was only in his mind. And so they kept climbing.

As Jonny got near to the top something odd began to happen. Mount Rumble started to become quieter, and there was less smoke in the air. With every step that Jonny took the volcano seemed to calm down, and with every step Jonny grew a little more confident. As he stepped onto the top of the volcano he saw the mouth of Mount Rumble shrink back, till it was no more than a little crater. The top was suddenly calm and cool, and the air was sweet. Dig and Keggle stepped up there and looked around.

'Where's the volcano?' asked Dig, almost sounding disappointed.

'Having a rest,' said Jonny, which was all he could think of to say right then.

Jonny walked across the top and looked down over the far side of the mountain. And as he did so he got a shock. There below, surrounding the base of Mount Rumble, was a seething, restless army of fog soldiers. And at the head of it was a single figure, taller than the others. It was the Fog Prince. Every head in that restless army was raised and every face was looking up at Jonny. It was as if he was looking at them through a telescope because he could see every snarling face, every sneering expression. They were all angry and arrogant down there. The Fog Prince was laughing too. And mouthing something at Jonny. He seemed to be calling out the words 'Give up!' as he did his mocking. Jonny felt a chill run through him. They were trapped on Mount Rumble. If the volcano didn't get them then the Fog Prince would. It was a desperate moment. Jonny shivered, he reached to wrap his coat around him but of course, he had no coat. He started to shake a little.

'What are you looking at?' It was Keggle, standing there beside him, at the top of Mount Rumble looking down.

Dig joined him. 'Yea, what's going on? ' he said.

They looked down the mountain but said nothing. Then Jonny realised.

'Can you see them?' he asked, pointing to the Fog Prince and his army of sneering fog soldiers down there.

'See what?' asked Dig. 'Look, is there anything to eat up here? Only I'm starving. There's nowhere to fish, and those rock pools stink, all sulphur and chemicals. No shellfish or crabs or nothing.'

Chapter Twenty Two

As Dig was talking a multi-coloured cloud of fog fell from the sky and engulfed them. Jonny could make out faces as he looked into the vivid, coloured swirls, but these weren't sneering, these were his friends. The fog friends from the other side of the-door-with-no-frame. Jonny felt suddenly better, stronger. Then he heard a familiar voice and felt a big hand on his shoulder. He turned to see a wise, smiling face looking at him. It was Dook.

'Dook! Am I glad to see you,' said Jonny.

'Am I glad to see you too,' said Dook. 'There are all kinds of stories going round back home about what's been happening. I was worried about you. I brought you this, 'cause they say it's so cold here.'

Dook held out a new coat for Jonny. It was bright and vibrant and very thick. Jonny pulled it on and immediately felt better. They sat down and Jonny told him the story so far. They chatted about the old times, back on the other side of the-door-with-no-frame and Dook told him how things were going there since he'd left. They laughed and bantered for a while, and all the time Dig and Keggle just stared in amazement. Then Firebreath Slimetongue the dragon came blundering out of nowhere, knocked Dig and

Keggle over and circled around everyone for a while. Eventually Dig came over.

'Jonny? This is cool,' he said. 'Who are these guys?'

He looked around, there were fog people everywhere. They were picking up handfuls of dirt and making new things with them. One of them fashioned a football and a clutch of them began to kick it around.

'We have to celebrate,' Dig said. 'Let's have a...'

As Dig was still talking the volcano suddenly shook, lightning split the sky and thunder cracked overhead. Then a roaring wind came from the south and blew so hard at them it might have been trying to whisk them off the mountain. Dig grabbed a rock and Keggle hung onto Dig. Jonny dug his hands and feet into the ground and let the wind pound his body as it blew past. As it died away the rushing sound melted into a kind of whispering. Like a strong, small voice. It was a bit like his dad's voice back home, as if he was passing by and breaking into Jonny's dream somehow.

'Well done, son, you're doing a great job. Don't give up. Keep going.'

Dig and Keggle looked up towards the night sky, they'd obviously heard it too. When they looked down again the fog people had gone. Firebreath had vanished too. Jonny looked around for Dook but he was nowhere to be seen. He felt his shoulder, it was still warm where Dook's hand had been on it. Jonny took a deep breath and stood up.

'Okay,' he said. 'Time to go back down.'

'Back down?' said Dig. 'Why? This place is much better than the mess down there.'

'We can't stay up here forever,' said Jonny. 'We just came up so we could go back down again.'

Keggle scratched his head. 'Eh? Really?' he said.

'Sure,' said Jonny.

'But can't we just hang around up here a bit longer?' said Dig. 'I could cook up a right stormin' stew with all these vegetables.'

'What vegetables?' asked Jonny.

Dig pointed around. The surface of the volcano was dotted with all kinds of vegetables left behind by the multi-coloured fog people.

'Be good and tasty,' said Dig.

'I bet it would be,' said Jonny, 'but if we stay here much longer Mount Rumble'll spew lava all over us.'

They looked over to the mouth of the volcano, smoke was seeping from it and the mouth was growing bigger again.

'Come on!' yelled Dig, 'Let's get outa here! Quick!'

They sped back down Mount Rumble and leapt into the boat. The Fog Prince and his men were nowhere to be seen now. They made it back across the water with no further signs of the lime green creature or the inky octopus, and the sea was fairly calm. But as they came out of the boat and tramped up the beach Miriam ran towards them. Her face was red and she was looking worried.

'Quick! Where've you been?' she gasped.

'We just had an amazing time!' said Dig.

'Yea, you should have been there,' said Keggle. 'It was awesome!'

'Well that's all right for you,' Miriam said, 'but you've got to come with me now! Quick!'

'What do you mean?' asked Jonny.

'It's Rooster,' she said.

'Oh not him!' said Dig. 'Complaining again is he?'

'You've got to help him. Please!' Miriam's eyes were wide with fear.

'Why? What's happened?' Jonny held Miriam by the shoulders and looked her straight in the eyes.

'The king - he did it. You know - the one you call the Fog Prince,' she said and she grabbed his sleeve and pulled on it.

Jonny started to run. Miriam was by his side. Dig and Keggle broke into a run too and went after them up the beach, their feet scuffing the sand as they went.

Chapter Twenty Three

Rooster was lying in a heap on the sand. Joey was sitting nearby looking miserable. There was a crowd of onlookers gathered there in the dark.

'We tried to help him but it was too late,' said Joey. 'Maybe if you'd been here the king wouldn't have got him.'

'What happened?' said Jonny, kneeling down and nursing Rooster's head. His face was deathly white and his fringe fell back revealing lifeless, staring eyes.

'Come on, don't just sit there, do something!' said a voice in the crowd.

'Yea,' said another, 'do a bit of your magic.'

Jonny looked up at the faces, they were all staring down at him expectantly. He recognised some of the folks he had met walking along the beach. Jonny shoved his hands under Rooster's limp body and picked him up. He was surprisingly light. He started to walk towards a nearby cave. They all followed him.

'No,' he said, 'everyone stay back. Just Miriam, Dig and Keggle.'

'Ohhh!' The crowd moaned and started complaining.

'That's not fair!' one of them said.

'Why do they get to go?' called out another.

'We don't want to miss the show!' said someone.

'It's not a show,' said Jonny and he kept walking towards the cave.

The crowd kept calling out and when Jonny looked back he saw them following. There were more of them than he had first thought. Suddenly Jonny felt angry. He had felt better after meeting Dook on Mount Rumble, but this was getting to him.

'Stay back!' he snapped at them.

'Why?'

'Because!' said Jonny and he walked into the cave.

Keggle, Dig and Miriam went in with him but the crowd loitered near the door. Others began to join them and it was getting noisy out there in the dark. Jonny laid Rooster carefully down, then sat him upright.

'Miriam, take off his coat,' he said.

'What?'

'You heard me, take off this old coat of his,'

Rooster's coat was dirty and ragged. He had obviously dragged it through plenty of mud at some point. They wrestled it from his shoulders and Miriam pulled it clear. Jonny laid him down again and stood up. He began to remove his own new, gleaming coat. The one Dook had just given him.

'Wow! That's a beautiful coat,' said Miriam as Jonny handed it to her. She didn't ask where his other one had gone. The one she had made for him.

'Put it on Rooster,' Jonny said to Miriam.

Miriam knelt down and Keggle helped, they lifted him up to a sitting position again and eased the new coat over his arms and around his body. Then they laid him down.

Outside the crowd had grown quiet. There was a strange hush in the air.

Jonny knelt beside Rooster and placed his hand on his eyes, then he pressed it over his mouth for a moment. Then Jonny stood up and took a step back. Nobody else moved.

Jonny cleared his throat. Then he said,

'Wake up Rooster!'

And someone in the crowd giggled.

'He's not having a nap!' they said.

Miriam turned and shushed them fiercely.

'Rooster!' snapped Jonnny, 'Wake up!'

Rooster didn't budge. He just lay there on the cave floor. His skin deathly white, his eyes staring, his lips a strange purple-grey colour. Jonny wondered what he should do now. Sometimes in this dreamworld he felt like he could do anything. But at the moment he was a bit unsure. He tugged at Rooster's cold hand and shivered, Jonny realised he was starting to feel cold again too. He spotted Rooster's old coat lying in a heap on the floor. Jonny had an idea. It just popped into his head. Jonny picked it up. It didn't smell great and looked even worse. Jonny shook it, held it up and slipped his arm into one of the sleeves. Then Rooster sighed. The quietest of sighs. He pulled on the other sleeve of Rooster's old coat and said again, 'Rooster, wake up!'

And Rooster opened his eyes. Suddenly he gasped and sucked in so much air his chest rose up really high. He coughed and spluttered and his eyes bulged wider than ever, Jonny pulled on the coat and knelt beside him. He lifted his head and Rooster looked at him as if Jonny was a stranger.

'Welcome back,' Jonny said with a grin.

Rooster said nothing. Outside the cave the others began chattering excitedly.

'We need to give him something to eat,' said Jonny.

A little boy wandered into the cave with a tiny piece of a stale doughnut.

'Don't give him that,' said Miriam.

'It's okay,' said Jonny. 'Wait a moment.'

Jonny took the doughnut, covered it with his other hand and held it for a moment. Then he uncovered his hand and revealed a new, fresh cake. He handed it to the boy.

'You give it to Rooster,' he said.

The boy smelt the cake and looked a little disappointed to be giving it away.

'Don't worry,' said Jonny, 'there are more here. Look.'

He pointed to a nearby rock and the boy's eyes burst wide as he saw a pile of fresh doughnuts just sitting there. The boy passed the one in his hand to Rooster, who took it and nibbled cautiously on it. Miriam took a clutch of the other doughnuts and passed them to the crowd outside the cave. The chattering grew louder. Before long they were all munching on the fresh cakes, and there was jam and sugar spilling everywhere.

'How d'you do that?' called a voice in the crowd.

'Yea, that was well cool.'

'Hey, why not turn this huge rock into a fat, juicy chocolate cake?'

One of the crowd brought in a large grey rock and dropped it at Jonny's feet.

'Go on, that'd be brilliant!'

Jonny looked down at the rock. He could imagine it there now as a big, tasty chocolate cake. He looked up, all the faces of the crowd were pressed together, looking in at the cave mouth, peering right at him. He glanced at Miriam who was standing beside him. She was frowning a bit. He looked back towards the faces again and caught sight of a few wisps of grey fog floating across the beach behind the crowd. He shook his head.

'No,' he said.

'Ohhhhh.' The crowd groaned and they all started moaning.

'Why not? You could do it.'

'Yea, go on.'

'Pleeeeeeaaaaase. Please, please, pleeeeeeeeeeeeeeeeaaaaassse.'

Jonny caught sight of the foggy wisps again. He shook his head a second time.

'It's a trap,' he said.

Chapter Twenty Four

Jonny looked at Miriam again.

'How did Rooster get hurt?' he said quietly.

She shrugged. 'He got mugged,' she said. 'He went off on his own and came limping back muttering about the king and his men. Then he collapsed on the beach.'

Jonny looked down at Rooster. He was smiling now and sitting up. He gave Jonny a hug, which wasn't like him really.

And at the same moment there was a shout outside the cave. People began running about and screaming. Dig and Keggle and Joey stood between Jonny and the mouth of the cave, forming a wall.

'What's going on?' said Jonny.

He looked over Keggle's shoulder. He could see the Fog Prince walking into the cave towards them. He was followed by a crowd of his dark, smoggy men.

'What do you want?' Jonny asked.

The Fog Prince didn't say anything. He just raised his hand. His long, jagged, broken-nailed finger pointed right at Jonny. Dig bent down, picked up a rock and hurled it at one of the prince's men. The figure yelped and grabbed his ear. Dig picked up another rock and raised his fist to throw it. But Jonny grabbed his hand from behind.

'No!' Jonny said. 'We can't win like this. There are too many of them.'

Dig looked confused and stared back at Jonny.

'Besides,' said Jonny. 'I have another plan.'

Dig slowly lowered his fist and let the rock fall. The Fog Prince's men sneered at them and pulled out long lumpy sticks. They raised them to hit Dig and the others, but Jonny's friends dived out of the way. The Fog Prince laughed and seemed to somehow move in an instant, because he was suddenly right beside Jonny, grabbing him by the shoulder. He signalled to two of his men and they swooped onto Jonny and took an arm each. Dig and Keggle and Joey started towards them again but the Fog Prince spat on the ground and a jet of flame shot up from nowhere. Jonny's friends leapt back. The Fog Prince's men raised their sticks again but Dig and the others didn't wait around, they shoved their way through the crowd of soldiers and barged their way back to the beach. On the sand it was cold and dark. The crowd of people had vanished. Dig looked up and down the beach and saw the boat in the distance. He ran for it with Keggle and Joey on his tail.

'It was a trap, wasn't it?' Jonny said quietly to the Fog Prince. 'You knew I'd help Rooster.'

'He wasn't really that sick you know. You're not that clever really,' said the Fog Prince shoving his face right up to Jonny's, 'I only gave him a sleeping potion.' His breath smelt foul. 'Oh and this.'

The Fog Prince reached for Rooster and pulled a canvas purse from his pocket. It jangled, obviously full of coins.

'I paid him well for his services. Didn't I Rooster?'

Rooster said nothing. The Fog Prince threw the purse back at him and turned to his men.

'Get this loser out of here,' he called, 'we need to finish this once and for all.'

The fog soldiers grabbed Jonny and hauled him out of the cave. As they pushed him along the beach they jabbed him with their sticks and called him names, cackling as they went. They seemed to think it was very funny to be able to push Jonny around now.

The Fog Prince followed them, rubbing his dirty hands together as he went.

Miriam and Rooster came out of the cave a few moments later.

'I was stupid wasn't I?' said Rooster.

Miriam shoved him. 'You were more than stupid!' she said. 'What were you thinking?'

'I dunno. The king offered me loads of money. And he's big and scary. Anyway, Jonny's bigger, he can handle it. He pulled Keggle out of his grave. He'll finish the Fog Prince for good now.'

But as they watched there was no sign that Jonny was handling it at all. The night was full of the sounds of the Fog Prince's men, cackling and shouting at Jonny. But they couldn't hear Jonny saying anything at all.

Slowly, quietly, Miriam and Rooster started to follow them. In the distance, behind them and in a boat on the sea, Dig, Keggle and Joey were rowing after them.

Part Three – Inside the Castle

Chapter Twenty Five

Jonny felt scared now. Really scared. It felt as if his dream was out of control. Like it was no longer his. As if someone else was dreaming about him and he was stuck with whatever was going to happen. Maybe he would never see his home again. Maybe he would never get back to reality. He felt the strange force of the fog soldiers shoving him along. Like he was caught in a vast spider's web, a million strands sticking to his arms and legs, moving him, trapping him, whisking him along. As if he was on an endless, unstoppable conveyor belt. Taking him where he did not want to go. And yet, also, in the back of his mind, he remembered that time on Mount Rumble with Dook and Firebreath Slimetongue and his other friends. And he remembered the unexpected sound he had heard - that sound from the sky. Like his father's voice telling him it was going to be okay. 'Well done, son, you're doing a great job. Don't give up. Keep going.'

He thought about those words again and again as the Fog Prince's men cackled at him and forced him to keep moving. He took a quick glance back. It was still very dark. It was still deep night, but he thought he could make out a couple of figures following them, a long way off. Then one of the soldiers jabbed him with his stick and he had to look forwards again.

Miriam and Rooster crept along. They could not see Jonny any more, just the crowd of fog soldiers. In the dark the soldiers looked like a big, ominous storm cloud, floating along the grey sand. Somewhere inside that cloud was Jonny, swallowed up by the king's evil intent. They were scared for him, but they kept following.

Out on the sea Dig and Keggle and Joey were in the boat, fighting the waves and doing their best to row after Jonny too. Suddenly Joey stood up and jumped out into the water. It came up to his chest.

'What are you doing?' Dig hissed at him.

'I'm sorry Dig,' Joey said, 'I can't do this. I gotta go.'

'Go where?'

'Somewhere quiet. Somewhere away from all this.'

'You can't abandon Jonny,' Dig hissed at him. 'We can help him.'

Joey looked towards the beach and that hovering, pulsating, evil cloud of soldiers.

'There's... there's... too... too m-m-many of them,' said Joey, and he started to shiver in the water, his teeth chattering, making it hard to speak. 'T-t-t-too m-m-m-many.'

And Joey turned away from the boat and began swimming towards the shore, away from Jonny. Dig looked at Keggle.

'What about you?' he asked. 'You going too?'

Keggle looked at the soldiers, then at Joey, then back to Dig. He nodded. Then he dived into the water and swam for his life.

Dig grabbed the oar he was holding more tightly and dug it into the water.

'Well, I'm not running away,' he muttered through gritted teeth. 'I'm never going to run away. Never.'

And he rowed on into the night, slowly closing the gap on Jonny and the fog soldiers.

Dig was the kind of boy who often made a mess of things. That was because he did lots of things and sometimes they went right and sometimes they went wrong. What you might call the law of averages. As he rowed into the night, following that crowd of fog soldiers, he was determined to get it right this time.

On the beach, further ahead, Rooster and Miriam slowed up. They were approaching a huge castle built of sand. It was a giant of a building and it towered above them. It had turrets and spires and domes all over it. Two massive sandy doors swung open and the fog soldiers swarmed through them and into the castle, taking Jonny with them. Then, quicker than they had expected the doors swung to again and slammed shut, showering bits of grit and sand over Rooster and Miriam as they loitered in the dark nearby.

'Who'd build a castle out of sand?' Miriam said. 'I've never seen it here before.'

'Well it's logical,' said Rooster, 'when you think about it. We've never been this far along the beach before. And the king can do anything he likes so if he wants to live in a massive sandcastle, why not?'

Miriam walked up to the doors and jabbed one of them. Her finger went right through.

'Don't do that!' said Rooster, 'you'll get us into trouble. There's another way in.'

'How d'you know that?' she asked, snapping her head round to stare at him.

Rooster shook the fringe so it covered his eyes and said nothing. Miriam jabbed her finger at him now.

'You've been here before, haven't you?' she said.

Rooster said nothing.

'You have, haven't you?'

Miriam reached for Rooster's pocket and pulled out the canvas purse.

'You came here to get this, didn't you?' she said. 'When you were plotting with the king to get Jonny. That's when you came here before. It's true, isn't it?'

Rooster still said nothing. He just snatched the purse back and began to walk around the castle. In the dark the sand looked very grey.

'Come on,' he muttered to Miriam and he kept walking.

She followed him around the side of the massive structure until he stopped and pointed to a tunnel entrance in the wall.

'We crawl in through there,' he said. 'It's not far.' He smiled. 'Then we can rescue Jonny.'

'We wouldn't need to rescue Jonny - if you hadn't betrayed him,' said Miriam.

Rooster said nothing more. He just crouched down, got onto his hands and knees and crawled inside. Miriam had no choice but to follow.

Watching them from a distance, as he dragged the boat out of the water, was Dig. This was his chance. Now he could be the hero and save the day.

Chapter Twenty Six

Inside the castle, in a huge shadowy arena, the Fog Prince stood with his jagged, dirty finger pointing at Jonny.

A large circle of evil, restless fog soldiers surrounded them both.

'You betrayed me,' the Fog Prince snarled.

But Jonny just quietly shook his head. And somewhere up above a little trickle of sand drifted down, a few grains dislodged from the castle walls.

'This world was mine, I made it,' said the Fog Prince.

And once again Jonny shook his head quietly.

And once again a little trickle of sand fell.

'We were partners and you walked away,' said the Fog Prince.

Once again Jonny shook his head quietly.

And once again a little trickle of sand fell.

'DON'T KEEP DOING THAT!!!!' the Fog Prince yelled, shoving his face right into Jonny's.

Around them both the circle of fog soldiers cackled and snarled too. But Jonny said nothing. The Fog Prince stepped back, took a deep breath, and calmed himself.

And a trickle of loose sand drifted onto his shoulder. He brushed it off, barely noticing.

Miriam and Rooster found themselves in a dark alley. The walls were solid sand and the alley snaked round a bend and out of sight.

'Follow me,' Rooster hissed, and he set off.

Miriam followed.

And behind them Dig emerged from the tunnel, caught sight of them disappearing and followed too. The alley was dark and they kept brushing their shoulders against the sandy walls. Bits of grit flew up and doused them as they hurried and at one point Dig tripped and hit the wall so hard he got a face full of sand. He stopped to wipe the grit from his eyes so he could see again. When he opened his eyes and could see clearly there was no sign of Miriam or Rooster. And the alley split in two up ahead. Which way should he go? Right or left?

'We used to be friends,' the Fog Prince said sadly. 'Why are we enemies now?'

'I'm not your enemy,' said Jonny and the Fog Prince look startled at the sound of Jonny's voice.

One of the soldiers stepped forward and jabbed him with his stick.

'Don't talk back!' he said.

'You told your friends to attack me didn't you?' said the Fog Prince.

Jonny frowned and shook his head. More sand trickled.

'YOU DID!' shouted the Fog Prince. 'You told them to kill us all.'

He swung his jagged finger around, pointing at the rest of his men.

'These are my true friends. They do everything I say. Those friends of yours are useless. That Dig idiot, always tripping over his own feet. That grinning fool Keggle. He has a big mouth, happily telling everyone you were going to come along and make things better again. They are better! Or they were till you started ruining things. Thanks to those traitors, Miriam and Joey. All of them. They're all fools and the sooner they're gone the better. And they will be - very soon. First I'll deal with you, then I'll deal with them. Then I'll do what I like. I'll go back through that door with no frame and make everything mine. EVERYTHING! EVERYTHING!' The Fog Prince was foaming at the mouth as he stomped up and down and shouted at Jonny. 'Rooster, he's the only one with any sense. He knows you can't win, Jonny. He knows you're a loser.' He shoved his face close up to Jonny's again. There was sweat and spit all over the Fog Prince's face. 'YOU'RE A LOSER!!!' he yelled.

Chapter Twenty Seven

Rooster and Miriam shuffled into the arena where they were questioning Jonny. They snuck in just in time to hear the Fog Prince say, 'Rooster - he's the only one with any sense. He knows you can't win, Jonny. He knows you're a loser.'

Rooster shuffled back into the shadows and looked at his feet. Miriam stood still and stared hard at him. He waved his hand at her.

'Come out of the light,' he hissed.

'There is no light here, it's all darkness,' she said. Ragged torches burned around the walls, but they only gave off a dim, dirty, orange glimmer. It was all strange and shadowy in there.

Rooster grabbed Miriam's shoulder and pulled her back, close to the wall. Trickles of sand drifted down and landed on them both. Rooster brushed sand from his hair, but Miriam didn't notice, she was looking at Jonny now. He looked so small and weak in the middle of the circle of those fog soldiers. They all held clubs and sticks and were jabbing Jonny with them. The Fog Prince yelled his last insult and then turned away and stepped out of the circle. He raised his long, dirty fingers and snapped them, and as he did the fog soldiers closed in on Jonny and hit him with their sticks. It was a terrible sight and the awful sound echoed around the arena.

Rooster looked up at the noise and watched with his mouth wide open. Miriam held up her hand to block out the sight. Rooster coughed and said, 'I think I made a mistake.' His voice sounded very dry and hoarse. Miriam looked around. The sound of Jonny being knocked about went on. She longed to run and stop them but she knew it would do no good. Instead she stared at one of the dark orange torches flaming on the side of the castle walls. The flame was dim and weak and seemed to be dying as she watched, but it gave her something to fix her eyes upon. Rooster however was walking away from her.

'Don't do this,' he was calling out.

The Fog Prince swung round to see who dared to interrupt the proceedings. He smiled when he saw Rooster.

'Well done,' the Fog Prince said. 'You did a good thing.'

Rooster shook his head and raised his voice.

'No I didn't! DON'T SAY THAT!!' he shouted suddenly. 'STOP THIS - IT'S HORRIBLE!!'

The Fog Prince's eyes drew wide, and he looked startled for a second. Then he burst out laughing. Yellow fumes seeped from his mouth as he flung it wide open.

'It's too late,' he said, pulling a huge, wide-mouthed grin.

Rooster reached into his pocket and pulled something out. He weighed it in his hand then raised his fist and hurled it at the Fog Prince. It was the canvas bag full of silver. It shot through the air like a rock, sailed through the Fog Prince's open mouth and out the other side of his head. The Fog Prince gulped for a second and his jaws clamped shut. There was the sound of jangling as the bag hit the floor behind him and the silver spilled out. He turned and looked at the money. Then he slowly turned back and snarled at Rooster.

'You stupid little boy,' he said through his gritted teeth. 'For that you'll pay like the rest of them. That injury I gave you so you could trap that loser will be nothing compared to what will happen now. You're all dead. You hear? DEAD!!!'

Dig blundered on down the narrow sandy passage. Every so often his shoulders scuffed the walls and clouds of sand flew up. From time to time sand fell from above too making it hard to see the way ahead. Eventually he found himself in a small, square courtyard. A few fog soldiers were standing around with sticks, talking quietly. When he blundered in they turned to look at him. Dig suddenly panicked, it felt like everything had gone completely wrong. He'd come to rescue Jonny, but Jonny wasn't here. Just some mean-looking soldiers, waving clubs and sneering at him.

'Oi!' one of them shouted. 'What you doing in here?'

'Er...' Dig's knees felt like they might give way and send him sprawling onto the floor. 'Nothing. Just... looking around.' he muttered.

'For what? That Jonny loser? He's dead mate!' And they all laughed.

Dig found himself joining in with their laughter.

'No way,' Dig said. 'That waster? Why would I be looking for him?'

One of the soldiers, the shortest and thinnest one, came up close to Dig and looked him in the eye.

'Because...' he wagged a stubby black finger in Dig's face, 'because you were with him back there at the cave. On the beach. I saw ya!'

Dig panicked. 'No. No. No. Not at all,' he said. And he gave a sneer as if he was impersonating them.

The little soldier jabbed him with his stick. He was much smaller than Dig who could probably have knocked him over with a sneeze.

'You sure?' he said.

Dig just nodded. The soldier walked back to the others, but they were all still staring at Dig. Suddenly the ground shook, and a tumble of sand fell from the walls. Dig turned and ran.

Chapter Twenty Eight

As the Fog Prince circled round Jonny in the huge, dark arena, Jonny remembered how it used to be in his dream. He remembered making the fog people, and Shimmersteel the unicorn, Firebreath Slimetongue the dragon, Rocktail the dinosaur. He remembered making the boy and the girl, and the world they created together. And he remembered hearing his dad's voice on Mount Rumble. He remembered all those good things. And then he remembered the war. That big battle between the Fog Prince's people and his people. Enemies that used to be friends. And he remembered Dook. And as he remembered Dook, he saw him there, in the castle, standing near the Fog Prince and about to grab him, right there inside this dark arena. And Jonny saw that there were others with Dook too. Other fog friends waiting to help Jonny fight the Fog Prince. But the plan Jonny had formed flashed through his mind so he looked at them and shook his head. The Fog Prince noticed and looked around, but he could not see Dook or Jonny's fog friends. So he turned back and just sneered at Jonny. And above them all, sand continued to rain down in ever thicker trails and trickles. The Fog Prince held up his hand and watched the sand pile up in his palm.

'What's going on?' he muttered, but no one answered.

Jonny looked at Dook again and shook his head a second time. Dook looked back sadly, but he didn't attack the Fog Prince. Instead he backed off and melted away through the walls along with Jonny's other fog friends. Jonny felt totally alone.

The Fog Prince snapped his fingers and his men suddenly transformed into a hundred cloudy grey snakes, hissing and spitting and closing in on Jonny. Two of them wrapped themselves around Jonnys' arms, stretched them out and pressed him back against the castle wall. Two more slithered around his feet, crossing over as they went, and they pinned his legs together. The others began to wrap themselves around the rest of his body, ready to squeeze the life out of him. The arena was filled with the sound of hissing and slithering. Then the Fog Prince snapped his fingers and the place fell silent. All the snake heads turned to him for a moment.

'Finish it,' he said.

And with a horrible ear-piercing hissing sound the snakes began to squeeze the life from Jonny as he was pressed there, arms splayed out, against the castle wall. More sand began to fall from the walls and the ceiling, and a tremor ripped through the floor.

'I don't understand,' said Miriam, 'Jonny could do anything. He made food out of nothing and he pulled Keggle from his grave. Why can't he do something now? Why can't he stop this?' Her words trickled away as she stared in horror at what was happening to Jonny.

Rooster stepped forward again.

The Fog Prince looked down as his feet rippled on the shaking ground.

'What's going on?' he said again, but no one answered. He heard someone yell 'No!' from behind and he spun round and pointed at Miriam and Rooster. Rooster was shouting at the snakes, trying to stop them.

'Get them,' the prince yelled, and two of the snakes broke free from Jonny and transformed back into fog soldiers.

They started towards Miriam and Rooster but a sudden, heavy tumble of sand fell from the roof in front of them and they were stopped dead in their tracks.

Jonny began to feel very strange as the snakes closed in around him. He felt really lonely and he felt as if he couldn't breathe too well, as if the walls were closing in on him. Pictures of some of the sad things that had happened in that land beyond the-door-with-no-frame flashed before his eyes. He wished he could break out of the dream again. Stop the whole thing and forget it all. He wished he could hear his dad's voice like he had on Mount Rumble. He wished Dook was there to put a reassuring hand on his shoulder. He wished he'd never fallen asleep and started this thing in the first place. But he did nothing about it now. He would not stop what was taking place.

And then something else happened. He began to feel as if he wasn't there at all. Instead he was looking down on himself from above. Like a camera in a film panning upwards above the scene. He could see himself and he looked small and frightened down there, and Jonny didn't like looking like that. Not at all. It all seemed wrong, very wrong. As the camera panned further up he could see more and more of the castle. His body and the snakes that were wrapped around him grew smaller and smaller, and now he could see the alleys and corridors and the ramparts and gateways. He saw Miriam and Rooster running for their lives. He saw Dig wandering the corridors looking lost and miserable. The camera went higher and he saw the whole of the castle now, and more. The beach it was on, and the land around it, looking all broken and full of litter. He could see the sea and Mount Rumble. The volcano was spitting fire and rocks and looking very angry indeed. The whole land looked old and dark and dirty. And it was shaking. The sand was kicking up in huge dust clouds that towered above everything else. Someone seemed to have hold of the land beyond the-door-with-no-frame, and they were shaking it up.

Miriam and Rooster burst out of the tunnel and sprawled on the beach. Rooster fell with his face in the sand. He leapt up spitting out the gritty, grey grains, and saw that Miriam was nearby dusting her hands and knees off. They did not know if anyone was following them but they didn't stop to find out. They ran and ran back across the beach, through the dust clouds and over the shuddering ground. Eventually they found Keggle and Joey hiding in a cave, so they huddled with them in the dark. Before long Dig appeared, not hurrying like Miriam and Rooster had been, but limping along, looking very sorry for himself. He snuck in the cave but didn't say anything. He just crept to the back and skulked in the dark there, away from the others. Looking out through the sandy haze and across the water they could just make out huge flames and massive burning rocks spewing out of Mount Rumble. Overhead the sky thundered and lightning kept cutting through the murk and zapping the sea. The water rose up and down like someone shaking a blanket violently. And the ground kept shuddering too. Nothing felt safe anymore.

'We're all going to die,' Keggle said.

'Yea, and it's your fault,' Miriam said to Rooster.

'Shut up,' said Rooster.

Dig said nothing. He just stared out of the cave into the dark sea. And there they stayed all night.

Back in the Fog Prince's sandcastle the walls were trembling. The more the snakes squeezed the life from Jonny, the more the place shook. The Fog Prince was starting to worry. He said nothing to his men, but he slipped out of the dimly lit arena and started running back towards the main exit. Piles of sand crashed around him as he went. In the arena the torches were going out one by one as they were doused by the crumbling sand from the walls and ceiling. The Fog Prince's men saw what was going on and began to recoil from Jonny. They changed from being snakes back into soldiers and they looked around for their leader. But of course he wasn't there. As they ran from the arena they found themselves trapped and buried in the falling corridors. The entrances were caving in and the castle itself was folding in on itself. The ground continued to shudder, pot holes opened up and the Fog Prince's men fell on their faces and were buried one by one.

And in the very centre of the Fog Prince's castle, still pressed into the wall with his arms outstretched, Jonny stood there silent and still. Bit by bit the arena fell in on him, and little by little his body was buried.

Chapter Twenty Nine

Jonny found himself walking alone. The castle had vanished and the dust clouds had simply disappeared. The day was clear and bright and he was back in the graveyard, where he had first met Dig and Keggle and Rooster. He caught sight of the lump of bread that Joey had thrown away. That seemed such a long time ago now. He reached down and picked it up, it should have been rotten and soggy now but it wasn't. It was fresh again. He heard heavy footsteps and turned to see a familiar creature bounding towards him.

'Rocktail!' Jonny called, and the dinosaur came up and butted him with his snout.

He split the lump of bread in two and shared it with Rocktail.

As they ate Jonny weaved his way between the old broken graves. The loneliness and terror he had felt in the castle had melted away now. And as he looked at the graveyard, lying there litter strewn and mashed up by the weather, he knew what he had to do. He felt confident again, his fears had melted away. He felt as if he could do anything right now.

He waved to Rocktail and clambered up onto the dinosaur's back.

'Come on, Rocktail,' he said. 'Roar at these graves for me. Shake 'em up a bit.'

Rocktail didn't question the order, he just threw back his head and let out an earth-trembling noise. Jonny had to cover his ears. As the roar died away the grave stones began to tremble. Then one by one they fell over and the ground covering the graves began to crack.

'Come on out!' called Jonny. 'It's time to live again.'

The ground was covered in a jigsaw of jagged lines as each grave began to split open. Here and there muddy hands shot up as if they were waving to Jonny.

'Come on!' called Jonny again.

The hands pushed higher, and arms and elbows appeared. Then shoulders and heads. Suddenly the graveyard was full of people pushing their way out of the ground. Before long they were standing there like a crowd of muddy football supporters. The bodies were dressed in their ragged clothes, the fabric torn and nibbled by the creatures that lived underground. But no one moved. They just stood and stared.

Jonny felt a breeze brush his cheek and he lifted up his hand.

'They need some air, Rocktail,' he said, 'they need some air in their lungs.'

And he began waving his hand like he was conducting an orchestra, ushering in the breeze, which soon became a rushing wind. It blustered around the graveyard, making the bodies dip and sway. Jonny had to cling onto Rocktail's back to avoid been blown off, his knuckles showed white with the effort. After a while the wind died down and the bodies stood still again.

'What now?' Jonny asked, but no one said anything.

Then he heard a cough. And another. And a gasp and a sneeze. One by one the bodies jolted and sucked in air. One by one they began to breathe again. They raised their dirty arms and stretched as if they were waking up from a good night's sleep. Some of them yawned noisily. One of them burped and another one laughed. They looked around at each other and a few of them let out a loud whoop. Suddenly the place was alive with shouting and laughter. The people began to tidy the graveyard, collecting up the bits of litter as they chatted and joked with each other.

Jonny watched them for a while but then suddenly felt very tired. So he left the crowd of people jumping and laughing and wandered on through the graveyard on Rocktail's back. They walked for quite a while and the graveyard stretched on. The voices died away and then Jonny spotted what he was looking for. A quiet cave. Right at the far end of the graveyard. He pointed to it.

'There, Rocktail,' he said, 'take me there. I need a lie down.'

Chapter Thirty

They woke up. Miriam, Joey and Keggle. Miriam rolled over to look at Dig. He was still sitting there in the cave staring out to sea. His eyes were sunken and dark, like little black ink wells. Miriam sat up,

'Where's Rooster?' she asked.

The others shrugged.

'I'll get some breakfast,' Dig suddenly said and he stood up and walked out towards the water.

Miriam noticed that the sky was clear. No thunder or lightning now. Mount Rumble was as quiet as a mouse, and the huge, hazy sand clouds had completely disappeared. She stood up and followed Dig out of the water. He crouched in the waves, getting soaked and doing his best to spot any fish. So far he had caught nothing.

'I'm going for a walk,' Miriam called to him.

Dig didn't reply, he just kept staring at the water. She glanced back towards the cave, Keggle and Joey were deep in conversation about something. She started walking. Her legs felt heavy and her feet dragged in the grey sand as she moved.

Jonny was sleeping. Dreaming within his dream. He was with Dook and they were back in the land beyond the-door-with-no-frame. The day was bright and cheerful and the place was full of creatures alive. In the distant sea sharks and dolphins cavorted in the water together.

'When did you come up with the plan?' Dook was asking Jonny as they walked.

'That day after the battle, when we found Rocktail dead. I wanted revenge but this idea sort of appeared in my head. You told me revenge wouldn't work. So I thought I'd go right into the trouble. Find out how bad it was, and that meant going where Rocktail had gone. Into the world of death. Into the stuff that the Fog Prince had created.'

Jonny shook his head and looked very sad. 'It was horrible in that sandcastle. Pressed against the wall by those slithering snakes. It felt as if they were squeezing the life from me, like I was losing every good thing I ever had. I was cold and everything was dark. No friends, just those sneering fog men. The Fog Prince wanted to ruin everything, and just so he could get his own way. I couldn't let him do that. So I fixed it. Sort of. I made it possible for dead things to live again.'

Jonny suddenly laughed. 'I kind of turned back time I suppose. In a weird sort of way. Reversed things a bit. It was horrible for a while. It was the worst thing ever. Ever.' Jonny shuddered. 'But afterwards, when I found myself in the graveyard with Rocktail it was the opposite. Like nothing was bad and everything was possible. Just seeing Rocktail alive again was fantastic. I knew I'd done it.'

Dook placed a hand on Jonny' shoulder. 'They'll go through the same kind of things, you know. Your friends. Miriam, Joey, Keggle, Dig. They'll face times when everything seems lost and horrible.'

'Yea, but also times when anything seems possible,' said Jonny, 'and maybe times when things seem dead, and then they come back to life again.' Jonny frowned. 'I wish I could make it so the Fog Prince never existed but I can't.'

'One day,' said Dook, and he nodded solemnly. 'One day.'

Then Dook placed his hand on Jonny's shoulder and shook him.

'What are you doing?' Jonny asked.

Dook didn't reply, instead he shook Jonny again, really violently. And then he did it a third time. Suddenly the world began to spin and Jonny felt like he was in a big washing machine, whizzing around.

The ground was shaking again. Then slowly things settled and came to a stop.

Jonny flicked open his eyes. The spinning sensation he had felt came to an end and he found himself lying in the cave. The cave he had walked to with Rocktail for a lie down. It was bigger than he remembered, the roof was a sloping arch and there were craggy piles of rocks here and there. Jonny was lying flat out on the hard, cold floor. There was a grating sound and he turned to see the huge rock covering the doorway roll away due to the ground shaking. The sun was shining outside and the warmth and the light crept in. Jonny sat up and stretched. He felt as if he'd been sleeping for a long time. In a moment everything came back to him, flashing before his eyes like a film on fast forward. The big crumbling castle, the Fog Prince, the clouds of sand, Rocktail and the graveyard, and then his conversation with Dook. And now here he was, back in this cave. He stood up and wobbled a little. His legs felt stiff and wooden, he shook them both and stretched them. He waited a few moments to get his strength and his balance back.

Then he heard soft footsteps. Cautious, hesitant. He recognised them immediately. He stood up and stepped towards the cave opening. He knelt down and slipped his head around the rock so that he could take a look outside. There she was. Miriam, walking slowly towards the cave. She looked sad and lost, as if she was walking but didn't quite know where she was going. As Jonny watched she came to a standstill nearby, perched on a rock and turned so she was facing away from the cave and out to sea. And then Jonny heard another sound. She was crying. And talking softly to herself.

'Why did we let him down? Why did it all go wrong? Why didn't he fix things?' She said these questions to herself over and over as Jonny listened. After a while he couldn't wait any more. He slipped out of the cave and tiptoed across the sand. He loitered right behind Miriam and, as she sat there, mumbling and crying quietly, he reached out and tapped her on the shoulder. She leapt up and spun round. But Jonny couldn't resist jumping the opposite way so he was behind her again. Somehow he knew which way she was going to turn and he dodged her.

'Who's there?' she called out and Jonny tapped her on the shoulder again.

She spun round but Jonny dodged her again.

'What's happening?' she called out.

Jonny tapped her a third time and this time he stayed exactly where he was so that when she spun round she was suddenly face to face with him.

'What? Who? Wh... what's going on? Who are you?'

He smiled but she was confused. He was the last person she expected to see so she couldn't work out who this stranger was.

'Miriam,' he said, with his eyes wide and excitement in his voice. He threw his arms open. 'It's me! Jonny!'

And suddenly she got it. Her eyes burst wide too and her mouth dropped open.

'Jonny? Really? You?'

'Yes!' He laughed. 'Me! Honest!'

'But... but... but... how? I mean, you... you... you... you weren't... how? You were... gone,' she stammered. Then before Jonny could answer her Miriam leapt at him and gave him a massive hug.

Chapter Thirty One

Miriam came splashing through the sea towards Dig. She was out of breath and gasping something at him.

'What?' he said. He was annoyed because he'd still not caught any fish.

'You'll never guess what!' she spluttered.

'Then you'd better tell me,' he said, 'and let me carry on with my fishing.'

'But you're not fishing. You haven't caught anything,' said Miriam.

'I will do, just give me time.' Dig went back to staring at the empty sea.

'Guess who I've just seen,' said Miriam.

'I thought you told me I wouldn't be able to guess,' said Dig.

'Jonny,' said Miriam.

'Jonny what?'

'Jonny!' said Miriam. 'I've just seen him.'

'You can't have done, The king captured him. He got buried in that castle. He's gone.'

'Wrong!' said Miriam. 'He's up the beach, back there.'

She wagged her thumb over her shoulder. 'I've just seen him by a cave.'

Dig took one look at her. Opened his mouth to speak, then snapped it shut again. He turned away from Miriam and shouted towards the cave.

'Keggle!' he yelled. 'Come with me!'

And Dig tore through the water, making huge splashes as he went. Keggle started running up the beach following him. They met on the sand and ran like mad towards the huge cave in the distance. Miriam shook her head and started walking back up the beach.

He wasn't there. Keggle got there ahead of Dig, but he paused at the cave mouth and Dig, with his usual bluster just pushed past him and went straight on in. The cave was empty. No sign of Jonny. Dig came back out and looked around. There were footsteps in the sand but no other sign. Keggle walked slowly into the cave and knelt down, tapping at the ground.

'You know what this means?' said Keggle.

'What do you mean?'

'If Miriam saw him here and now he's gone…'

'Yea?'

Keggle stood up. 'He's back.'

'Back?' said Dig, screwing up his face. 'Back where? He's not here.'

'So he's somewhere else,' said Keggle, and he pushed past Dig and walked back up the beach.

Dig looked around for a while, he felt a bit stupid. Didn't know what to do now. He stood there whistling for a bit, then instead of walking back to the others he looked towards the sea and decided to try fishing again. He waded into the water and stood around, trying to grab any passing food. Nothing. The sea was still empty. Someone shouted to him. Keggle probably. Or maybe even Rooster. He ignored it. Then another shout rang out. He looked towards the beach, there was a distant figure back there. Definitely looked like Rooster. Dig ignored it.

There was another shout. It was definitely Rooster out there on the sand. Dig was sure of it. Wherever he'd been all night he was back there now on the beach, yelling at Dig, trying to tell him what to do. Well, Dig didn't need help. He knew what to do. If there was one thing Dig knew about, it was how to catch fish.

'Try further over,' Rooster called.

'Don't be stoopid,' Dig called back without looking at him.

'I'm serious, try over there.'

Dig sighed and spat in the water. Rooster was starting to annoy him. He stayed where he was for another five minutes. Still he caught nothing. He glanced up. Rooster was still there, pointing to a nearby spot in the water.

What did Rooster know about fishing? Nothing. That's what. He should just get lost. Dig stared at the water for another long while. Nothing. No fish at all. He glanced over to the spot that Rooster was pointing to, he sighed, and waded over towards it. He stopped a couple of times on the way to see if he could spot fish anywhere else. Nothing. Eventually he went to the place Rooster had indicated. Immediately he spotted two huge fish, just idling there, swimming between his legs. He reached down immediately, grabbed them both and held them over his head in triumph. And in the same moment he realised. It wasn't Rooster on the beach there. It was Jonny. He'd done it again - given Dig some free food. Dig almost dropped the fish as he started running for the shore. He had to stop and juggle with them for a few moments. Jonny was standing there laughing at him.

Dig slowed up. His feet sloshed in the shallow water, they suddenly felt very heavy.

'It's okay,' said Jonny. 'I made a fire, look. We can cook breakfast.'

There was a healthy blaze not far away, all ready for roasting fish. Dig threw the fish on and they were soon sizzling and filling the air with a delicious smell. Keggle, Joey and Miriam appeared, no doubt hungry for some breakfast too. They were amazed to see Jonny again, and a little bit nervous too. They didn't say much at first, then as they relaxed and ate the delicious food together they started chatted noisily and asking lots of questions. Dig didn't say much though. He just sat there eating quietly.

Then Jonny sprang up. 'Dig, let's go for a stroll,' he said.

'I saw you running away in the castle,' Jonny said, as they walked.

'Did you? I...' he didn't know what to say, so he shut up and they walked in silence for a while.

Dig swallowed hard and said, 'I meant to help, that was what I wanted. I never planned to run... but I got lost... and there were solders... the king, I mean the Fog Prince... he was well scary...'

'I know. You weren't ready, that was all. But I think you are now.'

Dig stopped walking and looked at Jonny.

'Ready for what?' Dig felt suddenly scared again, like he had felt that night in the sandcastle.

'I need your help,' said Jonny. 'And they do too.'

Dig glanced back to see Keggle, Miriam and Joey wandering along behind them. They stopped suddenly and did their best to pretend they weren't following when Dig looked back. But it was obvious really.

'Dig you can do it,' Jonny said. 'Don't be intimidated by the Fog Prince. He's a full time liar. He and I used to be good friends, but not now. He's doing his best to mess up this world I made. I need you to help me rebuild it. Make it better. Won't be easy. But you can do it, I know you can. You and Keggle and Joey and Miriam. But they need someone to be in charge. Someone to lead them.'

Dig looked back at the others, they were wandering about on the sand, still pretending not to be following.

'You lead them,' he said. 'You lead all of us.'

Jonny shook his head.

'I can't stay around, Dig. It'll soon be time for me to go back.'

Dig turned and stopped Jonny, slapping a big hand on his chest.

'Don't be stoopid. You have to kill the Fog Prince.' Dig had raised his voice, was almost shouting. 'You have to.'

But Jonny shook his head. 'Doesn't work like that Dig. You're stuck with him for now. But he knows he's beaten. One day I'll finish it, I'm sure.'

'Finish it now,' said Dig, panic in his eyes. 'Finish it now.'

But Jonny shook his head again. 'Come on,' he said, 'let's keep walking.'

For a while Dig said nothing more. Jonny glanced back and caught sight of Miriam. She looked unhappy, she'd obviously heard what they'd been talking about.

'Joey annoys me,' said Dig eventually, 'I don't like the way he eats.'

Jonny laughed. 'Everyone annoys someone,' he said.

'What do you want us to do?' Dig asked.

'Look around you Dig, it's a mess. Look at it. It needs some folks to sort it out a bit. It's nothing like the place I first thought of.'

Jonny waved his hand over the beach. There were oily slicks smearing the dirty grey sand, and piles of cans and broken glass, along with streaks of grimy, torn clothes. Here and there mad mist people sat in a fog-like trance, staring out to sea.

'Why don't you do it?' Dig said. 'You could just snap your fingers and make it better.'

Jonny thought for a moment or two. 'No. It'll only get messed up again. And what do I do then? Keep snapping my fingers? Be better if I had friends like you to help me.'

'Where will you be?'

Jonny thought for a moment.

'I think I have to go back to my own world, Dig. Back to a place called Dagenham Drive.'

'What about Rooster?'

Jonny frowned and shook his head. 'Not sure. I need to talk to him, I need to track him down.'

'Is he okay?'

Jonny shrugged.

'I'll just sink again,' Dig said suddenly, and behind him Keggle laughed.

'What?' said Jonny.

'You know. Like in the water. I'll start going and I'll just sink again.'

Jonny laughed. 'Course you will. Everyone falls over sometimes. But at other times you'll be okay. Will you do it?'

'You should ask Keggle, he's nicer than me. Or Miriam. She's better. She's more reliable.'

Jonny shoved Dig in the shoulder. 'I'm asking you, Dig. Will you do it?'

Chapter Thirty Two

Dig looked at Jonny for the longest time. It was a big question, would he help Jonny? Could he help Jonny? He didn't want to rush the answer. Jonny waited. The sea rose and fell in the background. Joey, Keggle and Miriam stood nearby watching him. Eventually Dig nodded his head slowly. He would. If he could.

Jonny turned back towards the others. They looked small and worried. Jonny went over to them. 'I have to go now,' he said.

'NO!' yelled Miriam.

'I have to,' he said, 'but...' then Jonny had an idea. 'Hold out your hands,' he said.

He reached into his pocket and took out a small black box. He blew on it and placed it on Miriam's open palm. Silver wisps of breath seemed to form into a tiny hologram of planet earth inside the box as time slowed for a second. Then the lid closed and the hologram was gone. Jonny reached into his pocket a second time and took out another box and placed it on Joey's palm. He opened it and blew into that one too. Another hologram appeared for a second. He did this for each of them, blowing sliver wisps of breath into each little black box.

'Those boxes have a bit of me in them now,' Jonny said. 'I blew my energy into them. A bit of my life.'

Joey flipped up the lid of his box and frowned. But there's nothing here,' he said.' It's empty.'

'No it's not.' said Miriam.

Joey looked into her box, it looked the same as his – empty.

'There's nothing in it,' he said.

'Not everything can be seen with your eyes,' said Jonny. 'Some things are invisible. You can't see the wind can you? Only what it does. Can't see the internet, only the things it provides.'

Miriam nodded but Joey looked confused.

'You'll see it, when you need to,' said Jonny. 'You all will. I'm sure.'

Jonny went round and said goodbye to each of them. He felt suddenly really sad. He'd only known them a short time but it felt much longer. Dig didn't look at him as he said goodbye. He just stared at the ground and kept clearing his throat. Keggle had a single tear running down his cheek. Joey just chewed his lip. Miriam wasn't afraid to cry, and when she hugged him Jonny cried too. Then he stepped away from them, gave a quick wave and turned to walk away.

He wasn't finished yet though. He had one last thing to do.

Rooster did not know where he was. He had walked around in circles all night and he was now lost. He could not get the images out of his mind. The pictures of Jonny being attacked by the fog soldiers. It was horrible. And it was his fault. His foot kicked against something and he looked up. He was standing in front of a huge mountain of sand. Turrets stuck out at odd angles. It was the king's huge sandcastle, all collapsed and barely recognisable. And suddenly it hit Rooster. Jonny must still be in there. He needed rescuing. Rooster started scrabbling at the sand with his fingers, trying to dig a way into the massive pile. It was hard work but he wouldn't stop. Maybe this would fix things. Maybe this would make him feel better again. If he could just find Jonny and pull him out to safety. He dug and dug and dug. He was making quite a deep tunnel when he heard laughter behind him. He spun round, sand all over his hands. There was more laughter, the cackling kind. It was the king. Or the Fog Prince as Jonny called him. He was covered in grit and sand and his purple leather coat was very messed up. His boots were dirtier than ever, they were spattered with oil and seaweed.

'What do you think you're doing?' the Fog Prince asked.

'N... n... n... nothing,' said Rooster. He flicked the fringe from his eyes for a moment. It fell straight back and covered his eyes again.

'Doesn't look like nothing,' said the Fog Prince. 'You ruined my home.'

'What?'

'My castle. This is my home. Look at it now.'

'Wasn't me... it was...'

'Yes?'

'It was... well... Jonny... sort of...'

The Fog Prince suddenly stooped down and shoved his dirty face right into Rooster's.

'DON'T EVER say that name again!' he snarled. 'That fool is gone. Got it? GONE!'

'I know...' said Rooster. 'It was my fault.'

'Oh yes it was. Exactly!' said the Fog Prince. 'It was all your fault. So what are you doing here now?'

'I want to make it right,' said Rooster. 'I want to rescue him.'

The Fog Prince threw back his head and roared with laughter.

'You have no hope of that!' he said.

The Fog Prince extended his dirty fingers and beckoned to Rooster with his broken, jagged nails.

'Come on, you have to come with me now.'

But Rooster shook his head and turned back to his digging. He started working on his tunnel again. Behind him the Fog Prince's face turned dark grey. His body swelled up like a huge, dark storm cloud. Lightning cracked around his head. He reached out with his jagged fingers and was about to grab Rooster by the neck.

'You can't have him,' said a familiar voice, very quietly and very calmly. 'You can't have him.'

The Fog Prince spun round. It was Jonny. He was alive and well and standing right there.

'What?' snarled the prince.

'You heard me. You can't have him.'

'Jonny!' Rooster spun around and couldn't believe his eyes.

The Fog Prince turned even darker. More lightning cracked around his head.

'You are finished!' he yelled at Jonny, but Jonny shook his head.

'No,' Jonny said, 'you're the one who's finished. Rooster is safe with me. You can't have him. You tried to get rid of me and you couldn't do it. You failed.'

Chapter Thirty Three

The Fog Prince drew himself up to his full height, his eyes flashed like blazing buildings, and a streak of lightning shot out of his mouth towards Rooster. At the last moment Jonny put his fist in the way and deflected the shot. There was a sizzling sound as the fire hit his hand, and a curl of smoke rose up, but Jonny didn't flinch.

'You can't hurt him,' Jonny said.

The Fog Prince threw back his head and shrieked. Foul green smoke poured from his mouth. Then he cleared his throat with a horrible growling noise and spat a ball of phlegm way up into the sky. The putrid orange-green wad flew up and hovered above them, growing in size as it hovered in the sky.

Smoke began to pour from the foul wad and lightning crackled at its edges. The Fog Prince lifted his jagged hand and snapped his fingers. His nails were so sharp that he cut himself as he did it, and blood dripped across his palm and down his wrist. As the snap sounded in the air the horrible ball began to drop down out of the sky towards Rooster. As it fell it picked up speed and began to make a screeching noise. Dirty yellow lightning streaked behind it. Rooster screamed and crouched down, covering his head with his hands. But Jonny didn't move. He kept his eyes fixed on the foul missile, waiting for that last moment, when it would come close enough to do something about it. Jonny's foot swung back as he prepared his timing, then he leapt in the air and swung his foot right at Rooster's head. But instead of kicking Rooster, he connected with the falling missile just as it was about to hit Rooster, and he booted the thing as hard as he could. There was a terrible slurping sound and the huge smoking wad shot off Jonny's foot and went spinning out into oblivion. The Fog Prince let out an ear-shuddering shriek.

'Stop doing that!' he yelled and he fell on his knees.

But Jonny wasn't listening, he was grabbing Rooster by the arm, and throwing him over his shoulder. Then without looking back at their enemy, he carried Rooster away from the old castle and left the Fog Prince snarling on his knees, pounding the beach with his fists.

'I'm not finished yet,' he called after them. 'I'M NOT FINISHED YET!'

Jonny said nothing. He just kept walking.

Eventually, when they reached a quiet part of the beach Jonny placed Rooster down. Rooster collapsed in a heap and lay with the side of his face pressed against the sand, staring out to sea.

His eyes unblinking and fixed on the water. He was staring like one of the mad mist people.

'Are you all right?' Jonny asked him.

'I let you down,' Rooster mumbled, as if he was in a trance.

'That's past now, you can start again,' Jonny said. 'This is a new time.'

Rooster sat up and kept staring. The dirty grey sand was all over the right side of his face where he'd collapsed on the beach. He didn't brush it off.

Jonny looked at his shoe. There was slime all over it from the Fog Prince's missile. He began wiping his foot on the sand, cleaning off the mess and the awful-smelling goo.

'I can't,' said Rooster, 'I... I can't.'

'Can't what?'

'Start again. It was horrible what they did to you.'

Jonny nodded. 'It was horrible. It was really bad. Dead bad. I went to another place for a while.'

Jonny knelt down beside him and shook his shoulder.

'But it's gone now. Look at me. I'm back.'

But Rooster didn't look at Jonny. He just kept staring out to sea.

After a while Jonny stood up.

'It's up to you Rooster,' he said, 'go and find Dig and the others. They'll help you.'

Rooster shook his head. 'They hate me,' he said.

'No they don't, go and talk to them.'

'I can't,' Rooster said. 'I can't.'

'I have to go now Rooster,' Jonny said, 'I think my time's nearly up. Promise me you'll find the others.'

But Rooster didn't promise. He just kept staring out to sea.

Jonny turned sadly and began walking away. He glanced down at the burn mark on his wrist, the one from the Fog Prince's attack on Rooster. It hurt a bit, but not as much as leaving Rooster on the beach there. Every so often he looked back to see what Rooster was doing, but Rooster never moved.

Jonny strolled back towards the-door-with-no-frame. He felt tired now. Really tired. Here and there bits of litter flew past him, a sweet wrapper blew up and stuck to his chest and he had to push hard to brush it away. He passed one or two mad mist people but he decided not to stop. It was time for Dig and Keggle, Joey and Miriam, to sort them out now. His foot kicked against something and he looked down to see a broken grave stone. He stopped to look around.

He was in the graveyard, but all the graves were split open now. There were flowers growing here and there and the litter was gone. The people had broken out and were up and about somewhere, probably frightening their distant relatives by reappearing alive again. He heard the sound of Mount Rumble groaning in the distance and as he walked he passed through clouds of murky fog hanging in the air here and there. When he walked out of the last one he spied something in the distance. Something familiar, he moved towards it. The-door-with-no-frame. Standing there in the middle of nowhere. He walked up close to it and reached for the handle. He wondered if it would be hot to touch, but it was fine now. He turned it slowly and pulled open the door.

Chapter Thirty Four

As he hovered in the doorway he turned and took one last look behind him. Then he stepped through and turned back to close it behind him. And suddenly there was the jagged hand and soiled fingers of the Fog Prince - jabbing him right in the face, then grabbing him by the neck. The prince's face was covered in sweat and sand and muck. His lips were dark and contorted as he snarled at Jonny.

'You go back through that door and this world is mine! I'll destroy it all! You may have tricked me with your cheap scheming but you can't stop me doing what I want now! I'll wreck this place!'

'It's not your world,' said Jonny. 'It's mine. I made it and I'm gonna come back to it one day. So it had better still be here. You can't destroy it. I won't let you.'

The prince growled through gritted teeth and tightened his grip on Jonny's neck. He started to squeezed tightly and Jonny started to choke. He grabbed the prince's wrist and as he did the Fog Prince yelped and let go of him. He looked at his arm. It was smoking.

'What did you do?' asked the prince, looking confused.

'I died, remember? You buried me in your castle, and you thought I was gone and yet I came back. There's nothing you can do now. You've used up your power.'

The prince reached out to jab Jonny in the eye, but his finger stopped in mid-air as if it had suddenly hit an invisible wall. It hovered an inch away from Jonny's face and started to smoulder.

'Oww!' yelped the prince and he pulled his hand back and nursed it.

The Fog Prince rubbed his finger, narrowed his eyes and snarled at Jonny again. He looked as if he was trying to think of the next thing to do.

'Give up the fight, prince,' said Jonny. 'Stop causing trouble. You're going to lose.'

'I'm not a prince! I'm a king!' snapped the Fog Prince. And he turned and stormed off in a foul-smelling cloud of smog, lightning crackling around his head.

Jonny sighed and shook his head. He turned away, went back though the door and closed it behind him.

He was back in his own land. The air smelt sweet and there was no litter or rubbish strewn here and there. The place was full of colour and the sounds of life. Creatures and birds and old friends buzzed and ran around. He took a deep breath. And he felt a hand on his shoulder. He spun round to look, worried that it might be the Fog Prince again.

It was Dook, standing there with an encouraging smile.

'Welcome back Jonny,' he said, 'you made it. Am I glad to see you.'

Jonny smiled back.

'That was quite an adventure,' he said. Then he frowned. 'I'm still worried about Rooster though,' he said.

Dook Strong shrugged. 'It's up to him now. He has to make up his own mind. You did what you could Jonny. You did what was needed.'

'And all the others? D'you think they'll be okay?'

Dook knelt down and scooped up a handful of bright red earth. He made it into a tiny mountain in his hand and then pushed his finger into it to make a hole. As they watched a little plant grew up and spread its leaves. Dook tore a leaf off.

'You must be hungry,' he said.

Jonny chewed the leaf. It tasted like hot chocolate with marshmallows.

Dook ripped off another one and passed it over. Jonny scowled. 'Bacon sandwich. Hmmm. With hot chocolate and marshmallows?'

Dook laughed.

'Come on,' he said, 'let's go swim with some sharks.'

They spent the next hour diving and surfing in the waves, chasing the dolphins and the whales and the sharks. It felt like old times. Jonny had never been a great swimmer in his ordinary life, but here he could do anything. Afterwards he and Dook crawled up the beach and collapsed in a heap.

'You never answered my question about the others,' Jonny said sleepily as they lay dozing in the sun. 'Will they be okay?'

'They'll be a whole lot better for having you around,' said Dook. 'And me and the guys will be breaking through the-door-with-no-frame on a regular basis. You can count on it.'

Jonny nodded. 'That's... good,' he said slowly. 'Yes... good. And... and... and... one day... one day... I... I guess I'll go.... back... there... again...'

And he fell asleep.

Chapter Thirty Five

Jonny woke up. He flicked open his eyes and looked around. It was morning. He shut his eyes and flicked them open again. Yes. He was back. He was really back. He checked one last time. Shut his eyes, then opened them again. Faint sunlight streamed in though the gap in the curtains. He leapt out of bed and threw the curtains wide. Everywhere was white outside. It had been snowing in the night. And there was a gentle layer of mist in the air, hovering in the trees that lined Dagenham Drive. He stared at it for a while, thinking of Miriam and Joey, Rooster, Dig and Keggle. And Dook Strong and the Fog Prince. It had been quite a night. A huge dream. He felt a bit disappointed it was all over. But he remembered the sandcastle too, and the fog soldiers. He shivered even though his room was warm. He turned round. He saw the Star Wars lamp by his bed and all the usual things in his room. He was back. He was really back. He smiled to himself.

Then he remembered something else and ran to the end of his bed. There was the bright red sock, stuffed with strangely shaped objects. He reached inside and grabbed the first thing he could find. He tore the paper off. It was a large snow globe. He shook it up. Nothing that exciting about it really. But then he noticed something and looked closer. There were tiny figures inside fixed to the snow covered base, and in the middle a tiny free standing door-with-no-frame. On either side of the door the place was perfect. There was a tiny dinosaur and a unicorn butting each other, and a fire-breathing dragon nearby. The figures looked familiar too. They could have been Miriam, Dig, Keggle and Joey. As he shook it again the swirling bits of snow seemed to morph into figures. His old fog friends. No sign of the Fog Prince though, or his soldiers. But Dook was there, and before the figures faded away he thought he saw Dook Strong turn and wave at him. The world inside the snow globe was perfect. It wasn't grey, or dirty, or full of litter. Jonny looked at it for a long time and wondered what might have happened to Rooster. And then he spotted something. A tiny figure he'd not seen before. A fringe of hair covering the eyes. A peaceful smile on the small figure's face. Jonny smiled to himself again. Then he put it to one side, emptied out the Christmas stocking and began tearing open the other presents. It was Christmas morning, and the dreaming was over.

The Perfect Thai F

by Russ Crowley & Duangta Wanthong Mondi

Published by Russ Crowley

The Perfect Thai Phrasebook

www.learnthaialphabet.com

Copyright © 2014 by Russ Crowley

All rights reserved. No part of this book may be reprinted or reproduced or utilised in any form or by any electronic, mechanical, or other means, now know or hereafter invented, including photocopying and recording, in information storage or in an retrieval system, without permission in writing from the author.

ISBN 978-1-908203-15-1 (paperback)

ISBN 978-1496095770 (CreateSpace-assigned ISBN)

Translations by Duangta Wanthong Mondi

Read What Others Have Said About Our Products

I have achieved more than I would have thought possible in such a short space of time. Your colour code and picture aids make learning so much easier and it's so easy to refresh my memory from your app. I must say Russ, for me your product has been a great help, well worth the small price paid, and, would wholeheartedly recommend it to anyone wanting to learn to read and write Thai.

Orville Earle, London, UK, 17th October 2013

The Thai language is very intimidating and this program has taken the fear away! I would give it an 11 out of 10 points!! Thanks Russ!

Sandra Ching, Ecuador, 9th September 2013

I agree that your app and those posts are like a speed-of-light catalyst in terms teaching one the Thai script and reading it within literally two days (in my experience) which I find extraordinary!... I am just extremely excited that I have finally found material that does not throw one into the deep end of things.

Emiliusz Smorczewski, Illinois, USA, 9th July 2013

I have been very pleased with how quickly I have been able to learn and retain so much. Another aspect to purchasing is the quality of service received. The iPad version is awesome because I can use it anywhere without internet. I travel a lot and often am without internet, so it makes it nice.

Brian Atwell, USA, 3rd October 2013

Your teaching technique is very good, much better than the other books I've seen.

Julian Wheeler, Chonburi, Thailand, 28th October 2012

These resources are making the learning of Thai a reality after numerous false starts... the simplicity of the system breaks down the psychological barriers to attacking the idea of reading/writing Thai.

Brock Estes, Richmond, VA, 15th September 2012

Table of Contents

1. Welcome to QuEST 1
   - 1.1 What is Quest? 2
2. Introduction 1
3. Do's and Don'ts 3
4. Thailand, its Alphabet and Language 5
5. Tone 6
6. The Thai Alphabet 7
   - 6.1 Consonants 7
   - 6.2 Vowels 9
7. Politeness 11
   - 7.1 Particles 11
   - 7.2 Thank You 11
8. How to Use This Book 12
   - 8.1 What Do You Mean By That? 12
   - 8.2 Layout 13
9. Basic Formalities 16
   - 9.1 How to Introduce Yourself 16
   - 9.2 Making Friends 20
   - 9.3 Wish Someone Something 23
   - 9.4 Question Words 23
   - 9.5 Asking for Help and Directions 24
   - 9.6 Solving a Misunderstanding 25
   - 9.7 Determiners 26
   - 9.8 Pronouns 27
   - 9.9 Date and Time 27

9.10 Numbers	28
10. Welcome To Thailand	**28**
10.1 Customs & Immigration	28
11. Looking for Lodging	**32**
12. Where Am I Going...and How Do I Get There?	**38**
12.1 Getting Around Thailand	38
12.2 Getting Around Town	42
13. Culinary Considerations	**49**
14. Feeling a Little Parched	**53**
15. Seeking Souvenirs	**55**
16. I Should Have Brought More Money	**58**
17. I Have a Question...	**59**
18. Emergencies	**61**
18.1 In Case of a Little Emergency (At the Pharmacy)	63
19. The Kids Are Alright	**65**
20. Let's Go to the Movies	**68**
21. Where's the Party	**70**
22. Some Toilet Talk	**71**
23. Are you Traveling Alone?	**73**
24. Keeping Busy (Things to See and Do)	**76**
25. Life on the Wild Side	**77**
26. Learn a Little	**77**
27. Important Personages	**78**

Appendix 79

　　Appendix A.　Verbs　　　　　　　　　　　　80
　　Appendix B.　Adjectives　　　　　　　　　82
　　Appendix C.　Food and Cooking　　　　　83

Index 87

Bibliography 92

A Note From the Authors 93

1. Welcome to QuEST

Welcome to **QuEST**: *Quick, Easy, Simple Thai*, volume 3 - *The Perfect Thai Phrasebook*.

We believe that starting to learn a new language is akin to starting an adventure. With learning Thai, not only will this be an exciting journey into a foreign land, but it's an exploration into a country that is more than likely vastly different from that of your own; and, the mixture of trepidation and excitment you are perhaps feeling helps to make this both thrilling and unique.

Indeed, many peole baulk at the thought of trying to learn Thai script, preferring rather to concentrate on speaking and using transliterated Thai. All of this is fine of course – Thai's LOVE to hear foreigners speak, or try to speak, their language; but, by buying this book, you are not only committing yourself to wanting to learn more about Thailand's language, but you are showing you are interested in wanting to learn more about her country, her culture, and her people; and, this is a whole new adventure.

Indeed, setting off down this side-road will not only allow you to delve deeper into the essence of Thailand, but you will find that, as you continue to travel and the more you explore, you will be amazed at what lies around the next corne and is revealed as more paths open up before you – these series of small adventures then help to make up an entire *Quest - Quick, Easy, Simple Thai.*

1.1 What is Quest?

Quest is our methodology for teaching you Thai. Consisting of 4 volumes, Quest takes you from a beginner, with zero knowledge of the Thai language, through to being able to read Thai.

Volume I - Learning Thai, Your Great Adventure is the place to start your Quest. Introducing the Thai language, the alphabet: the consonants, classes and sounds, vowels, tone, why it's important; and so much more.

Volume II - Memory Aids to Your Great Adventure is the book that makes learning the Thai alphabet so simple: it couldn't get any easier.

Volume III - The Perfect Thai Phrasebook

Volume IV - How to Read Thai makes the process of breaking down Thai sentences into words, and words into syllables. Thai has few spaces and puntuation and the answer to the common question of, *"Where or how do you even start?"* is a mystery no longer.

Of course, learning the Thai alphabet is quite difficult for some and as there is no one size fits all teaching method, we also have *The Learn Thai alphabet application*, which is based on volume 2 of *Quest* and is web-based so it works on your PC, Mac and iPad. You can see more about this in section 8.2, starting on page 13 (or go to www.learnthaialphabet.com).

2. Introduction

Welcome to Thailand!

First of all, we appreciate you may not physically be in the Land of Smiles just yet, but by getting this phrasebook you are thinking of the future, of making that transition from where you are today, to where you will/or want to be; hopefully, this is not too far off. This book is designed so that you can read a bit about Thailand, it's history, people, culture and language, and then learn some very important basics which will make your trip infinitely more enjoyable: being polite, being able to introduce yourself, being able to make friends and a little bit of *go for it* – all in the Thai language.

Most people who have been on holiday abroad realise that being able to converse in the language of the country they're visiting makes one's own experiences infinitely more enjoyable – it's a fact; and, this book is all about giving you the tools to learn some simple, key, every-day phrases which will enable you to converse with Thai people on your trip and to make it that much more memorable. Thai's are very friendly and will assist you anyway, but showing them that you are trying to learn their language and their culture will definitely make them more inclined to assist you. We know of few people who have not wished they had made more of an effort to learn a few phrases before they visited a new country – this book gives you that chance.

Though there are a lot of phrases in this book, and certainly more than enough to ensure you get the most of your time in the kingdom, you must understand that learning a few phrases does not equate to learning the language. Indeed, some people have no desire to ever progress past the initial stage or of trying to make their time abroad infinitely more enjoyable, but that comes down to one's own personal choice; however, if you wish to put in that little extra effort and attempt to learn a bit more, the tools are here.

Initially, because of the unfamiliar script, you will need to use a Romanised version of Thai; this version is called *Transliterated Thai*. Transliteration tells you what you need to say in English to make yourself understood in any given situation.

All foreigners will use this at the first stage, you have to. The problem for the visitor is that not many Thai people understand transliterated Thai; it's not their language or script, so why would they? But, the added problem is because transliterated text is just 'a starter', the time spent learning it is effectively wasted. Of course, if your goal is to learn a bit more about Thai's and Thailand you could, and should, devote your time to actually learning the language itself.

3. Do's and Don'ts

If you're travelling to Thailand then regardless of the reason for your visit, you want to enjoy yourself. We won't go into details about drinking plenty of water, using lots of sun-screen, wearing a hat, carrying an umbrella, and that kind of thing, your guide book will provide most of that information. However, what we will emphasise is that Thailand probably has vastly different customs to your own country. Again, your guide book will probably cover it but we will just emphasise some of those you should pay particular attention to.

Most Thais are Buddhists, and in Buddhism the belief is that the head, as the highest point of the body, is to be respected; similarly, the feet - the lowest point - are the dirtiest. Consequently, never touch anyone's head without their permission (even a child) and, if you are invited to someone's house, or before you go into a temple, take your shoes off; don't take your dirt in with you. To do otherwise, in either circumstance, would be considered very rude. You do not need to remove your shoes before entering public buildings, shops and similar, but definitely for private dwellings and religious places. If you are unsure, just ask <u>before</u> you enter.

The King of Thailand is revered and loved by all Thais, so please pay the appropriate respect at all times. In addition, Thailand has strict *lese majeste* laws to further discourage disrespect. If you chose to visit a cinema on your stay in the kingdom, the Royal

Anthem is always played before the start of the main feature; please stand and pay your respects to the King.

The next part should go without saying, but I will mention it just to clarify - avoid confrontations! One key part of life in Thailand is the appearance of *'saving face'*. No-one ever wants to deemed insufficient, incapable, or any other factor, nor do they want to ever feeling, or be in a situation which causes them to lose face. Consequently, we would recommend that you avoid any situation where this is likely to happen; believe us, isn't worth it.

Russ has travelled quite extensively and says there isn't a single country that he has been to where he hasn't been ripped-off or scammed to one extent or another; sadly, this seems to be a part of life. No-one likes it, but if you ever find yourself in such a situation and feel you have suffered loss, just smile, say *mâi bpen rai* (page 17) and walk away. Afterwards, if you are genuinely upset or still grieved, contact your tour guide, your holiday rep or the [tourist] police (page 61), and lodge a complaint and/or ask them to assist. Whatever you do, don't start shouting and screaming, trust us, it won't work and you will more than likely lose – don't ruin your trip!

Other than that, be sensible, be polite, enjoy yourself, smile a lot, and treat others as you yourself would want to be treated.

4. Thailand, its Alphabet and Language

The official, national language of Thailand is Thai. Though there are various other related languages (some would call dialects) of *standard – or Siamese –Thai*, it is spoken by approximately 20 million people (Thai language, 2012).

Thai script is believed to have derived from Khmer, and the Thai alphabet was first created in 1283 by King Ramakamhaeng of Sukothai (Slayden, 2010). The alphabet consists of 44 consonants and 32 vowels (Crowley & Mondi, 2011) and is a tonal language. This means that word pronunciation is important as mispronouncing the tone will infer a different meaning; therefore, you must have an understanding of the tones.

The next sections briefly cover the main points of the alphabet, in particular:

- Tone
- Consonants
- Vowels

The next page shows the marks that we use to distinguish tone in transliterated text. These marks are different to the tone marks used in written Thai but these are beyond the scope of this phrase book. These are covered fully in *Quest Volume 1 - Learning Thai, Your Great Adventure*.

5. Tone

Every syllable in every word has one of five tones, these are: *Middle tone*, *Low tone*, *High tone*, *Rising tone* and *Falling tone*. In transliterated Thai, we write these as follows:

Tone	Tone Mark	Transliterated Thai Example
Middle	No tone sign	Gaa
You say this with your normal voice, constant pitch		
Low	\	Gàa
Your voice starts at a slightly lower pitch than your normal (mid tone) voice and dropping throughout.		
Falling	^	Gâa
Your voice starts higher than your mid tone, rises briefly, and then finishes lower than mid tone.		
High	/	Gáa
Your voice starts higher than mid tone and rising throughout.		
Rising	v	Gǎa
Your voice starts slightly lower than mid tone, drops briefly, and finishes high.		

6. The Thai Alphabet

In this section we will look at all the components of the Thai alphabet: the consonants, the vowels and the tone marks.

6.1 Consonants

As mentioned before, there are 44 consonants in the Thai alphabet. A summary of their attributes is as follows:

Thai Consonant	Sound	As In...
ก	/g/	galahad
ข	/k/	kangaroo
ฃ	/k/	karaoke
ค	/k/	koala
ฅ	/k/	koala
ฆ	/k/	kite
ง	/ng/	guarding
จ	/j/	jabberwocky
ฉ	/ch/	chat[2]
ช	/ch/	chef
ซ	/s/	saxophone

Thai Consonant	Sound	As In...
ฑ	/t/	typist
ฒ	/t/	tea-bag
ณ	/n/	navigate
บ	/b/	bald
ป	/bp/[1]	bottom
ผ	/p/	profit
ฝ	/f/	fruit
พ	/p/	pray
ฟ	/f/	finish
ภ	/p/	paint
ม	/m/	map

---

[1] In English, we don't have /dt/ and /bp/ as initial sounds.

[2] This is more of a /sh/ sound than a hard /ch/. Think cat in French: /ʃæt/

Thai Consonant	Sound	As In...	Thai Consonant	Sound	As In...
ฌ	/ch/	child	ย	/y/	yeti
ญ	/y/	you	ร	/r/	rabbit
ฎ	/d/	dog	ล	/l/	large
ฏ	/dt/[1]	dog	ว	/w/	wave
ฐ	/t/	tassle	ศ	/s/	sign
ฑ	/t/	tortoise	ษ	/s/	sea
ฒ	/t/	training	ส	/s/	squirrel
ณ	/n/	napoleon	ห	/h/	hump
ด	/d/	damsel	ฬ	/l/	look
ต	/dt/[1]	damsel	อ	/ɔɔ/	awful
ถ	/t/	tail	ฮ	/h/	hooray

The table above shows just the sound when the consonant is an initial consonant [in a syllable or word].

> *If you really want to learn the language then you need to get Quest Volume 1 -* **Learning Thai, Your Great Adventure***; and, if you want to progress to reading Thai, then you need either Quest Volume 2 –* **Learn Thai Alphabet with Memory Aids to Your Great Adventure***; or, if you prefer interactive learning,* **The Learn Thai Alphabet Application***; plus, you will need Quest Volume 4 –* **How to Read Thai***.*
>
> *All are available from* www.learnthaialphabet.com.

6.2 Vowels

Thai has 32 vowels in total, divided first into simple and complex vowels, and then further sub-divided into short and long versions of each. Naturally, Thai script shows everything, but differentiating between long vowels and short vowels can be difficult with some types of transliteration system. There are about 12 different transliteration systems in use in Thailand, but with the transliteration system we use – that developed by the *Paiboon Publishing Company* – short vowels are written with a single vowel and long vowels are doubled-up. For example a short /a/ vowel sound is written as 'a'; whereas the longer /aa/ vowel sound is written as 'aa'. Very simple, and very effective.

6.2.1 Simple Vowels

Short Vowel			Long Vowel		
Vowel	Sound	Sounds Like	Vowel	Sound	Sounds Like
The 4 vowels to the right can be short or long but are considered long for tone purposes.			̊ำ	/am/	umbrella
			ใ-	/ai/	knight
			ไ-	/ai/	fly
			เ-า	/ao/	mouse
-ะ	/a/	puffin	-า	/aa/	palm
̀ิ	/i/	lip	̀ี	/ii/	Steeple
̀ึ	/ʉ/	push	̀ื	/ʉʉ/	bloom
ุ̀	/u/	crook	ู̀	/uu/	boot
เ-ะ	/e/	net	เ-	/ee/	bed

Short Vowel			Long Vowel		
Vowel	Sound	Sounds Like	Vowel	Sound	Sounds Like
แ-ะ	/ɛ/	trap	แ-	/ɛɛ/	mare
โ-ะ	/o/	cot	โ-	/oo/	ghost
เ-าะ	/ɔ/	slot	-อ	/ɔɔ/	awful

6.2.2 Complex Vowels

Short Vowel			Long Vowel		
Vowel	Sound	Sounds Like	Vowel	Sound	Sounds Like
เ-อะ	/ə/	above	เ-อ	/əə/	early
เ-ียะ	/ia/	ria	เ-ีย	/iia/	reindeer
เ-ือะ	/ʉa/	newer	เ-ือ	/ʉʉa/	skua
-ัวะ	/ua/	buat	-ัว	/uua/	pure
ฤ	/rʉ/	rook	ฤๅ	/rʉʉ/	root
ฦ	/lʉ/	look	ฦๅ	/lʉʉ/	looney

As a very rough estimate, when you pronounce a long vowel, it is approximately 2-3 times the length of a short vowel. If you think of the difference between saying the letter 'n' in English, and then saying the letter 'm', this gives you an approximation.

QUEST: Quick, Easy, Simple, Thai

7. Politeness

Thai people - *kon* Thai (*kon* is both singular and plural and means both person and people) – are very friendly and the word you will hear the most whilst in Thailand will either be *kráp* or *kâ* (depending on whether you are listening to a male or a female).

7.1 Particles

These two words are polite particles and are used to make every sentence sound softer and more polite. If you watch Thai television or listen to Thai radio at all you will see presenters use these all the time, literally at the end of every sentence – no-one wants to appear rude.

Fortunately, the rules are very simple. Male speakers use *kráp* and female speakers use *kâ*. These aren't interchangeable and you should always use the correct particle in normal conversation.

Female	kâ
	ค่ะ
Male	kráp
	ครับ

> *Either particle can be used at the end of every sentence or phrase in this book; you can't be over polite.*

Another word you will also hear and see to make a sentence softer, is ná (นะ); it is frequently heard, especially when the listener is younger.

7.2 Thank You

Thai people are very polite and simply saying thank you for something makes a huge difference; it's also a good habit to get into. Using either of the following two phrases at the same time as a smile works wonders for everyone, and we're sure they will work for you too:

Thank you	kɔ̀ɔp kun
	ขอบคุณ
Thank you very much	kɔ̀ɔp kun mâak
	ขอบคุณมาก

8. How to Use This Book

Okay it's a phrase book. Have you ever been to a foreign country before and asked a question from a phrase-book? All is good until the native person you are asking the question of answers – then you're lost from the first syllable. The next recourse is to ask them to point to the phrase in the book…and so on .

Well, this phrase book is slightly different to other books you might be used to in that we only include the phrases you will actually need.

8.1 What Do You Mean By That?

Well, we all know there is a huge difference between what we write, and what we actually say; a phrasebook is the written version of what you should say. In this book, we aim to show you what you should say.

As an example, in Thai there are different expressions for good morning, good evening and good night (*à-run-sà-wàt*, *sǎ-yan-sà-wàt* and *raa-dtrii-sà-wàt* respectively); but, the most commonly used term is *sà-wàt-dii*.

Sà-wàt-dii is another word you will hear and use a lot on your vacation of travels in Thailand as it is very versatile. It means hello, but also has other meanings, such as: it is used to say goodbye; it can also perform the role of bidding someone good morning, good afternoon, good evening, and good night, all depending on the context of the address: if you walk into a restaurant in the early evening and say *sà-wàt-dii* then it's obvious you're not bidding the waitress goodnight. However, though it might be used in a more formal situation, where an informal departure is required, such as you've finished your meal and are leaving, a simple thank you, *kɔ̀ɔp kun kâ / kráp,* will suffice.

This is not to say we won't give you the other phrases, in some cases we will, we just think if no-one actually uses these expressions, then why try and teach you something you won't use. Of course, there may come a time when you do hear expressions like those mentioned above, but they are quite rare.

8.2 Layout

We've laid-out this book so that the English phrase you are looking for is on the left, and the transliterated text is on the same line.

Thank you	kɔ̀ɔp kun
	ขอบคุณ
Thank you very much	kɔ̀ɔp kun mâak
	ขอบคุณมาก

If it doesn't all fit, then it will wrap onto subsequent lines.

Directly beneath this is the Thai script you, or anyone else, can read. For example, you can point to it and the person then knows what you are trying to say.

If after your visit to the Land of Smiles, you really want to learn Thai, then a great place to start is with *Quest Volume 1 - Learning Thai, Your Great Adventure.* LTYGA explains the language system, the alphabet, how to speak, read and write Thai, and gets you learning the language, quickly, easily and effectively.

At the time we first wrote this Phrasebook (in November 2012), there were no other learn Thai language books that teach you to read Thai in full-colour with word-spaced and hyphenated Thai script – none; and, now almost 18-months later, there still aren't!

This may not sound like much, but imagine learning from pages and pages of block text, versus learning from coloured images, with the Thai script spaced for you, plus the transliterated Thai, and the English meaning all in one place: it's the best method we have come across to learn Thai.

Also, as Thai script is unfamiliar to all foreigners at first, to read Thai you must learn the script. Some people can learn via a tabular format (as in LTYGA), others will use flashcards and write it all down, and the rest will use an altogether different method, but they all have one thing in common – the methods are all slow and make learning the Thai alphabet hard work.

With volume 2 of *Quest – Learn Thai Alphabet with Memory Aids to Your Great Adventure (MATYGA)*, we make the learning process easy. By colour-coding pictures we help your brain learn in the way it likes to learn – with images.

In addition, we also have our *How to Read Thai* book, *volume 4 of Quest*. Again, a first of its kind, we guide you step-by-step through the process of learning to read Thai.

We break-down all those sentences, words and syllables enabling you to decipher and read Thai[3]. You can get the books at the following website:

http://www.learnthaialphabet.com

Also, if interactivity is your thing, we also have another first (we are ground-breaking in our material you know!), this time it's the electronic version of *Learn Thai Alphabet with Memory Aids to Your Great Adventure* and is simply called *Learn Thai Alphabet*.

All you need is a web-browser on your pc, Max or iPad and then you can learn the alphabet, test yourself, and really nail learning the alphabet wherever you are and quickly!

---

[3] You need to know the Thai alphabet, or be on the way to learning it before getting this book.

9. Basic Formalities

9.1 How to Introduce Yourself

Hi / Hello.	sà-wàt-dii
	สวัสดี
My name is...	chăn/pŏm chûu..
	ฉัน/ผม ชื่อ
What's your name?	kun chûu à-rai
	คุณชื่ออะไร
Mr. / Mrs. / Miss	naai / naang / nang-săao
	นาย.../ นาง.../ นางสาว
What is his / her name?	kăo chûu à-rai
	เขาชื่ออะไร
Welcome (to greet someone).	yin-dii-tôɔn-ráp
	ยินดีต้อนรับ
Could you please repeat that?	gà-rú-naa pûut ìik tii
	กรุณาพูดอีกที
How are you?	sà-baai dii măi
	สบายดีไหม
• Good (or, not bad)/So-so.	Gɔ̂-dii/ rûuai-rûuai
	ก็ดี /เรื่อยๆ
• I'm fine, thanks.	chăn/pŏm sà-baai-dii kɔ̀ɔp
	ฉัน/ผม สบายดี ขอบคุณ
• And you?	lɛ́ɛo kun là
	แล้วคุณหล่ะ

Basic Formalities

You're welcome / No problem / C'est la vie.	mâi bpen rai ไม่เป็นไร
It's nice to meet you.	yin-dii tîi dâai rúu-jàk ยินดีที่ได้รู้จัก
• you too	chên-gan เช่นกัน
Can you speak English?	kun pûut paa-săa ang-grìt dâi măi คุณพูดภาษาอังกฤษได้ไหม
Can you speak Thai?	kun pûut paa-săa tai dâi măi คุณพูดภาษาไทยได้ไหม
• Just a little.	nít-nɔ̀ɔi นิดหน่อย
• No, I cannot.	pŭut mâi dâi พูดไม่ได้
• Thai is easy / difficult.	pûut paa-săa tai ngâai / yâak พูดภาษาไทย ง่าย / ยาก
Please	gà-rú-naa กรุณา
Please speak more slowly.	gà-rú-naa pûut cháa gwàa níi กรุณาพูดช้ากว่านี้
Have you eaten yet?	gin kâao lɛ́ɛo rɯ̌ɯ yang กินข้าวแล้วหรือยัง
• Yes (I have eaten).	gin lɛ́ɛo กินแล้ว
• No (I haven't eaten yet). (Literally 'no eat' yet)	yang măi gin ยังไม่กิน

What country are you from?	kun maa-jàak bprà-têet à-rai
	คุณมาจากประเทศอะไร
• I am from...	chăn/pŏm maa-jàak...
	ฉัน/ผม มาจาก
− ...England.	ang-grìt
	อังกฤษ

pŏm maa-jàak ang-grìt means *'I am from England'*

− ...America.	ə-mee-rí-gaa
	อเมริกา
− ...Canada.	kɛɛ-naa-daa
	แคนาดา
− ...Thailand.	tai
	ไทย
Where do you live?	bâan kun yùu tîi-năi
	บ้านคุณอยู่ที่ไหน
• I live in...	chăn/pŏm yùu tîi bprà-têet
	ฉัน/ผม อยู่ที่ประเทศ
− ...England.	ang-grìt
	อังกฤษ
− ...America.	ə-mee-rí-gaa
	อเมริกา
− ...Canada.	kɛɛ-naa-daa
	แคนาดา
− ...Thailand.	tai
	ไทย

Basic Formalities

How long have you been in Thailand?	kun yùu tîi bprà-têet tai naan kɛ̂ɛ nǎi lɛ́ɛo
	คุณอยู่ที่ประเทศไทยนานแค่ไหนแล้ว
• I've been here for...	chǎn/pǒm yùu tîi nîi
	ฉัน/ผม อยู่ที่นี่
− ...days.	lǎai wan lɛ́ɛo
	หลายวันแล้ว
− ...weeks.	lǎai sàp-daa lɛ́ɛo
	หลายสัปดาห์แล้ว
− ...months.	lǎai dʉʉan lɛ́ɛo
	หลายเดือนแล้ว
Where are you going?	kun gam-lang bpai nǎi
	คุณกำลังไปไหน
• I'm going...	chǎn/pǒm gam-lang bpai
	ฉัน / ผม กำลังไป
It's really hot today (temperature).	wan-níi rɔ́ɔn jing-jing
	วันนี้ร้อนจริงๆ
I'm hungry.	chǎn/pǒm hǐo
	ฉัน/ผม หิว
I'm thirsty.	chǎn/pǒm hǐo nám
	ฉัน/ผม หิวน้ำ
I'm tired.	chǎn/pǒm nʉ̀ʉai
	ฉัน/ผม เหนื่อย
I'm hot.	chǎn/pǒm rɔ́ɔn
	ฉัน/ผม ร้อน

Good-bye / Cheerio / Goodnight. (this is common usage)	sà-wàt-dii สวัสดี
Good-bye. (not so common)	laa-gɔ̀ɔn ลาก่อน
See you later.	lɛ́ɛo jəə-gan mài แล้วเจอกันใหม่
Yes.	châi ใช่
No.	mâi ไม่

9.2 Making Friends

Where are you from?	kun bpen kon tîi-nǎi คุณเป็นคนที่ไหน
Where were you born?	kun gə̀ət tîi-nǎi คุณเกิดที่ไหน
• I'm from the U.S.	chǎn/pǒm maa-jàak ə-mee-rí-gaa ฉัน/ผม มาจากอเมริกา
• I'm from Thailand.	chǎn/pǒm maa-jàak bprà-têet tai ฉัน/ผม มาจากประเทศไทย
• I'm American	chǎn/pǒm bpen kon ə-mee-rí-gan ฉัน/ผม เป็นคนอเมริกัน
Where do you live?	bâan kun yùu tîi-nǎi บ้านคุณอยู่ที่ไหน
• I live in (the U.S / Thailand)	chǎn/pǒm yùu tîi bprà-têet ə-mee-rí-gaa / tai ฉัน/ผม อยู่ที่ประเทศอเมริกา/ไทย

Basic Formalities

Do you like it here?
kun chɔ̂ɔp tîi-nîi mǎi
คุณชอบที่นี่ไหม

Thailand is a wonderful country.
bprà-têet tai bpen bprà-têet tîi wí-sèet mâak
ประเทศไทยเป็นประเทศที่วิเศษมาก

What do you do for a living?
kun tam-ngaan à-rai
คุณทำงานอะไร

I work as a…
chǎn/pǒm bpen…
ฉัน/ผม เป็น

- …translator.
nák-bplɛɛ
นักแปล

- …businessman.
nák-tú-rá-kit
นักธุรกิจ

I like Thailand.
chǎn/pǒm chɔ̂ɔp bprà-têet tai
ฉัน/ผม ชอบประเทศไทย

I like the Thai language.
chǎn/pǒm chɔ̂ɔp paa-sǎa tai
ฉัน/ผม ชอบภาษาไทย

I've been learning Thai for 1 month.
chǎn/pǒm riian paa-sǎa tai maa nùng dʉʉan lɛ́ɛo
ฉัน/ผม เรียนภาษาไทยมา 1 เดือนแล้ว

Oh! That's good!
ôo dii mâak ləəi
โอ้! ดีมากเลย

How old are you?
kun aa-yú tâo-rai
คุณอายุเท่าไร

I'm (twenty, thirty...) years old.	chăn/pŏm aa-yú (yîi-sìp / săam-sìp) bpii ฉัน/ผม อายุ (20 / 30) ปี
How do you say [this] in Thai?	[nîi] paa-săa tai pûut yàang-rai [นี่] ภาษาไทยพูดอย่างไร
You're very kind!	kun jai-dii mâak คุณใจดีมาก
What's new?	mii à-rai mài bâng มีอะไรใหม่บ้าง
Nothing much.	mâi mii à-rai mâak ไม่มีอะไรมาก
Excuse me.	kɔ̌ɔ-tôot ขอโทษ
I'm sorry (apology)	kɔ̌ɔ-tôot ขอโทษ
I'm sorry (upset).	chăn/pŏm sĭia jai ฉัน/ผม เสียใจ
I'd like to visit England.	chăn/pŏm yàak bpai tîiao bprà-têet ang-grìt ฉัน/ผม อยากไปเที่ยวประเทศอังกฤษ
What are you doing?	kun gam-lang tam à-rai คุณกำลังทำอะไร
Say hi to John for me.	fàak sà-wàt-dii John dûuai ná ฝากสวัสดีจอห์นด้วยนะ
I have to go.	chăn/pŏm dtɔ̂ɔng bpai lɛ́ɛo ná ฉัน/ผม ต้องไปแล้วนะ

Basic Formalities

I will be right back.	chǎn/pǒm jà klàp maa mài ná ฉัน/ผม จะกลับมาใหม่นะ

9.3 Wish Someone Something

Good luck!	chôok dii โชคดี
Happy birthday.	sùk-sǎn wan-gə̀ət สุขสันต์วันเกิด
Happy New Year.	sà-wàt-dii bpii mài สวัสดีปีใหม่
Congratulations!	yin-dii dûai ยินดีด้วย
Enjoy your meal.	gin kâao hâi à-rɔ̀ɔi ná กินข้าวให้อร่อยนะ
This meal is delicious!	aa-hǎan mʉ́ʉ níi à-rɔ̀ɔi mâak อาหารมื้อนี้อร่อยมาก
Goodnight.	raa-dtrii sà-wàt ราตรีสวัสดิ์
Sweet dreams.	fǎn dii ná ฝันดีนะ

9.4 Question Words

Who?	krai ใคร
What?	à-rai อะไร

When?	mûua-rai
	เมื่อไร
Where?	tîi-năi
	ที่ไหน
Why?	tam-mai
	ทำไม
How?	yàang-rai
	อย่างไร
May I have a look at this?	kɔ̆ɔ duu nîi nɔ̀ɔi dâi măi
	ขอดูนี่หน่อยได้ไหม

9.5 Asking for Help and Directions

Help!	chûuai-dûuai
	ช่วย
I'm lost.	chăn/pŏm lŏng-taang
	ฉัน/ผม หลงทาง
Can I help you?	hâi chăn/pŏm chûuai măi
	ให้ ฉัน/ผม ช่วยไหม
Can you help me?	chûuai chăn/pŏm nɔ̀ɔi dâi măi
	ช่วย ฉัน/ผม หน่อยได้ไหม
Where is the bathroom?	hɔ̂ɔng-nám yùu tîi-năi
	ห้องน้ำอยู่ที่ไหน
Where is the pharmacy?	ráan kăai-ya yùu tîi-năi
	ร้านขายยาอยู่ที่ไหน
I'm looking for John.	chăn/pŏm gam-lang hăa John yùu
	ฉัน/ผม กำลังหาจอห์นอยู่

Basic Formalities

One moment please!	sàk-krûu
	สักครู่
Hold on please! (phone)	tǔɯ-sǎai rɔɔ sàk-krûu
	ถือสายรอสักครู่
Excuse me...! (to ask for something)	kɔ̌ɔ-tôot
	ขอโทษ
Excuse me! (to pass by)	kɔ̌ɔ-taang nɔ̀ɔi
	ขอทางหน่อย
Come with me (please).	(gà-rú-naa) maa gap chǎn/pǒm
	(กรุณา) มากับ ฉัน/ผม
Come with me!	maa gàp chǎn/pǒm sí
	มากับ ฉัน/ผม ซิ

9.6 Solving a Misunderstanding

I'm sorry (if you don't hear something).	kɔ̌ɔ-tôot, à-rai ná
	ขอโทษ อะไรนะ
Sorry (for a mistake)!	kɔ̌ɔ-tôot
	ขอโทษ
No problem.	mâi mii bpan-hǎa
	ไม่มีปัญหา
You can also use *mâi bpen rai*	mâi bpen rai
(it is far more common)	ไม่เป็นไร
Can you say it again?	chûuai pûut ìik kráng
	ช่วยพูดอีกครั้ง
Write it down please.	gà-rú-naa kǐian hâi duu nɔ̀ɔi
	กรุณาเขียนให้ดูหน่อย

I don't understand.	chǎn/pǒm mâi kâo-jai
	ฉัน/ผม ไม่เข้าใจ
I don't know or I have no idea.	chǎn/pǒm mâi rúu
	ฉัน/ผม ไม่รู้
I don't know (him / her / them).	chǎn/pǒm mâi rúu-jàk
	ฉัน/ผม ไม่รู้จัก
What's this called in Thai?	nîi paa-sǎa tai rîiak-wâa à-rai
	นี่ภาษาไทยเรียกว่าอะไร
What's that called in Thai?	nân paa-sǎa tai rîiak-wâa à-rai
	นั่นภาษาไทยเรียกว่าอะไร
What does 'riian' mean in English?	'riian' bplɛɛ wâa à-rai nai paa-sǎa ang-grìt
	'เรียน' แปลว่าอะไรในภาษาอังกฤษ
How do you say 'please' in Thai?	'please' nai paa-sǎa tai pûut yáang-rai
	please ในภาษาไทยพูดว่าอย่างไร
What is this?	nîi kɯɯ à-rai
	นี่คืออะไร
My Thai is bad.	paa-sǎa tai kɔ̌ɔng chǎn/pǒm yɛ̂ɛ
	ภาษาไทยของ ฉัน/ผม แย่
I need to practice my Thai.	chǎn/pǒm dtɔ̂ɔng fùk paa-sǎa tai
	ฉัน/ผม ต้อง ฝึกภาษาไทย
Don't worry.	mâi dtɔ̂ɔng bpen hùuang
	ไม่ต้องเป็นห่วง

9.7 Determiners

Thai language doesn't use *a*, *an* or *the*.

Basic Formalities

This / That / Here / There

nîi / nân / tîi-nîi / tîi-nân

นี่ / นั่น / ที่นี่ / ที่นั่น

9.8 Pronouns

I / Me (f / m)

chăn / pŏm

ฉัน / ผม

You

kun

คุณ

He / She, Him / Her

kăo

เขา

They / Them

pûuak-kăo

พวกเขา

We / Us

pûuak-rao

พวกเรา

9.9 Date and Time

Today / Now!

wan-níi / dĭiao-níi

วันนี้ / เดี๋ยวนี้

Tomorrow / Yesterday

prûng-níi / mʉ̂ɯa-waan-níi

พรุ่งนี้ / เมื่อวานนี้

What time is it?

gìi-moong lɛ́ɛo

กี่โมงแล้ว

It's 10 o'clock (in the morning).

sìp-moong

10 โมง

In the morning / evening / at night

dtɔɔn-cháo / dtɔɔn-yen / dtɔɔn-glaang-kʉʉn

ตอนเช้า / ตอนเย็น/ ตอนกลางคืน

9.10 Numbers

One, two, three	nùng, sɔ̌ɔng, sǎam
	๑ / ๒ / ๓
Four, five, six	sìi, hâa, hòk
	๔ / ๕ / ๖
Seven, eight, nine, ten	jèt, bpɛ̀ɛt, gâo, sìp
	๗ / ๘ / ๙ / ๑๐

10. Welcome To Thailand

10.1 Customs & Immigration

May I see your passport?	kɔ̌ɔ duu nǎng-sɯ̌ɯ dəən-taang nɔ̀ɔi
	ขอดูหนังสือเดินทางหน่อย
What is the purpose of your visit?	kun maa pɯ̂ɯa wát-tù-brà-sǒng à-rai
	คุณมาเพื่อวัตถุประสงค์อะไร
I'm a ...	chǎn/pǒm bpen…
	ฉัน / ผม เป็น

- …student. nák-riian
  นักเรียน

- …tourist. nák-tɔ̂ɔng-tîiao
  นักท่องเที่ยว

- …business traveller. nák-tú-rá-gít
  นักธุรกิจ

Welcome to Thailand

Where will you be staying in Thailand?	kun jà bpai pák-yùu tîi-nǎi nai mɯɯang tai
	คุณจะไปพักอยู่ที่ไหนในเมืองไทย
• I'll be staying in...	chǎn/pǒm jà bpai pák tîi
	ฉัน/ผม จะไปพักที่
– ...hotel.	roong-rɛɛm
	โรงแรม
– ...hostel.	roong-rɛɛm raa-kaa tùuk
	โรงแรมราคาถูก
– ...guesthouse.	bâan-ráp-rɔɔng
	บ้านรับรอง
– ...campsite.	sà-tǎan-tîi dtâng kâai
	สถานที่ตั้งค่าย
I need a tourist visa.	chǎn/pǒm dtɔ̂ɔng-gaan wii-sâa nák-tɔ̂ɔng-tîiao
	ฉัน/ผม ต้องการวีซ่านักท่องเที่ยว
I need a business visa.	chǎn/pǒm dtɔ̂ɔng-gaan wii-sâa nák-tú-rá-gít
	ฉัน/ผม ต้องการวีซ่านักธุรกิจ
I need a student visa.	chǎn/pǒm dtɔ̂ɔng-gaan wii-sâa nák-riian
	ฉัน/ผม ต้องการวีซ่านักเรียน
I need a retirement visa.	chǎn/pǒm dtɔ̂ɔng-gaan wii-sâa gà-sǐian aa-yú
	ฉัน/ผม ต้องการวีซ่าเกษียณอายุ

Do you have anything to declare?	kun mii à-rai tîi jà jɛ̂ɛng hâi sâap măi

คุณมีอะไรที่จะแจ้งให้ทราบไหม

- Yes.   kâ/kráp

ค่ะ/ครับ

- No.   mâi kâ/mâi kráp

ไม่ค่ะ/ไม่ครับ

Where are you coming from?	kun gam-lang maa-jàak năi

คุณกำลังมาจากไหน

Where is your Arrival card?	bàt pûu-dooi-săan kăa-kâo kŏɔng kun yùu tîi-năi

บัตรผู้โดยสารขาเข้าของคุณอยู่ที่ไหน

Where is your Departure card?	bàt pûu-dooi-săan kăa-ɔ̀ɔk kŏɔng kun yùu tîi-năi

บัตรผู้โดยสารขาออกของคุณอยู่ที่ไหน

Do you understand?	kun kâo-jai măi

คุณเข้าใจไหม

- Yes, I understand.   kâ/kráp chăn/pŏm kâo-jai

ค่ะ/ครับ ฉัน/ผม เข้าใจ

- No, I don't understand.   mâi kâ/mâi kráp chăn/pŏm mâi kâo-jai

ไม่ค่ะ/ไม่ครับ ฉัน/ผม ไม่เข้าใจ

Where is the immigration office?	săm-nák-ngaan dtrùuat kon kâo-mʉʉang yúu tîi-năi

สำนักงานตรวจคนเข้าเมืองอยู่ที่ไหน

Welcome to Thailand

I'd like to extend my visa.   chăn/pŏm yàak dtɔ̀ɔ wii-sâa
ฉัน/ผม อยากต่อวีซ่า

What time does the immigration office open?   săm-nák-ngaan dtrùuat kon kâo-mʉʉang bpə̀ət gìi moong
สำนักงานตรวจคนเข้าเมืองเปิดกี่โมง

- It opens at 08.30, but you need to get there very early.
bpə̀ət wee-laa bpɛ̀ɛt naa-li-gaa săam-sìp naa-tii dtɛ̀ɛ kun dtɔ̂ɔng bpai tǔng tîi-nân dtɛ̀ɛ-cháo
เปิดเวลาแปดนาฬิกา สามสิบนาที แต่คุณต้องไปถึงที่นั่นแต่เช้า

Please take a number and wait over there.   gà-rú-naa ráp bàt-kio lɛ́ɛ rɔɔ dâan nóon
กรุณารับบัตรคิว และรอด้านโน้น

Where can I get a photocopy made?   chăn/pŏm săa-mâat tàai săm-nao dâi tîi-năi
ฉัน/ผม สามารถถ่ายสำเนาได้ที่ไหน

Where can I get photos taken?   chăn/pŏm săa-mâat tàai rûup dâi tîi-năi
ฉัน/ผม สามารถถ่ายรูปได้ที่ไหน

Personal Details

First (given) name   chʉ̂ʉ
ชื่อ

Surname   naam-sà-gun
นามสกุล

Home address / ID Card Address	tîi-yùu dtaam bàt bprà-chaa-chon
	ที่อยู่ตามบัตรประชาชน
Address in Thailand	tîi-yùu nai mʉʉang-tai
	ที่อยู่ในเมืองไทย
• City	mʉʉang
	เมือง
• Province	jang-wàt
	จังหวัด
• Country	bprà-têet
	ประเทศ
• Nationality	săn-châat
	สัญชาติ
• Date of Birth	wan dʉʉan bpii gə̀ət
	วัน เดือน ปีเกิด
• Place of Birth	sà-tăan-tîi gə̀ət
	สถานที่เกิด

11. Looking for Lodging

I'm looking for a hotel near...	chăn/pŏm gam-lang hăa roong-rɛɛm tîi glâi gàp
	ฉัน/ผม กำลังหาโรงแรมที่ใกล้กับ...
• ...a beach.	hàat
	หาด
• ...a market.	dtà-làat
	ตลาด

Looking for Lodging

- ...clubs.   nai-kláp
  ไนต์คลับ

- ...restaurants.   ráan aa-hǎan
  ร้านอาหาร

- ...temples.   wát
  วัด

- ...bus station.   sà-tǎa-nii kǒn-sòng
  สถานีขนส่ง

- ...train station.   sà-tǎa-nii rót-fai
  สถานีรถไฟ

- ...airport.   sà-nǎam-bin
  สนามบิน

Do you have any rooms available?   kun mii hɔ̂ɔng wâang mǎi
คุณมีห้องว่างไหม

Do you have a shuttle bus?   kun mii rót ráp-sòng mǎi
คุณมีรถรับส่งไหม

I'm looking for a ... room.   chǎn/pǒm gam-lang hǎa hɔ̂ɔng sǎm-ràp...
ฉัน/ผม กำลังหาห้องสำหรับ...

- ...Single...   nùng kon
  1 คน

- ...Double...   sɔ̌ɔng kon
  2 คน

- ...Family...   krɔ̂ɔp-krua
  ครอบครัว

Can I see the room first?	chăn/pŏm kɔ̆ɔ duu hɔ̂ɔng gɔ̀ɔn dâi mǎi
	ฉัน/ผม ขอดูห้องก่อนได้ไหม
How much is it per night?	kʉʉn lá tâo-rai
	คืนละเท่าไร
Is the price per room or per person?	nân raa-kaa dtɔ̀ɔ hɔ̂ɔng rʉ̌ʉ dtɔ̀ɔ kon
	นั่นราคาต่อห้องหรือต่อคน
Is there a... in the room?	nai hɔ̂ɔng mii... mǎi
	ในห้องมี...ไหม

- ...safe... — dtûu sêep — ตู้เซฟ
- ...air conditioner... — krûuang bpràp-aa-gàat — เครื่องปรับอากาศ
- ...fan... — pát-lom — พัดลม
- ...bathtub / shower... — àang àap-nám / fàk-buua — อ่างอาบน้ำ / ฝักบัว
- ...hot water... — nám ùn — น้ำอุ่น
- ...fridge... — dtûu yen — ตู้เย็น
- ...bottled water... — nám dʉ̀ʉm — น้ำดื่ม
- ...TV... — too-rá-tát — โทรทัศน์

Looking for Lodging

- ...wi-fi...

    in-tîə-nét
    อินเทอร์เน็ต

Please don't bring... into the room.

    gà-rú-naa yàa nam ... kâo
    maa nai hôong
    กรุณาอย่านำ...เข้ามาในห้อง

- ...durian...

    tú-riian
    ทุเรียน

- ...outside guests...

    kon nôok
    คนนอก

- ...pets...

    sàt-líiang
    สัตว์เลี้ยง

I have a reservation.

    chăn /pŏm dâi joong wái lɛ́ɛo
    ฉัน/ผม ได้จองไว้แล้ว

Is breakfast included?

    ruuam aa-hăan cháo măi
    รวมอาหารเช้าไหม

I want a smoking room.

    chăn /pŏm dtôong-gaan hôong tîi
    sùup-bù-rìi dâi
    ฉัน/ผม ต้องการห้องที่สูบบุหรี่ได้

I want a non-smoking room.

    chăn /pŏm dtôong-gaan hôong tîi
    sùup-bù-rìi mâi dâi
    ฉัน/ผม ต้องการห้องที่สูบบุหรี่ไม่ได้

What time is check-in?

    kâo hôong dâi gìi moong
    เข้าห้องได้กี่โมง

What time is check-out?

    kʉʉn hôong gìi moong
    คืนห้องกี่โมง

Can I leave my luggage here until then?

chăn/pŏm gèp grà-bpăo-dəən-taang wái tîi-nîi jon-gwàa jà kâo hôong dâi, dâi măi

ฉัน/ผม เก็บกระเป๋าเดินทางไว้ที่นี่ จนกว่าจะเข้าห้องได้ ได้ไหม

Can you arrange a tour to... ?

kun chûuai jàt-dtriiam tuua bpai ... dâi măi

คุณช่วยจัดเตรียมทัวร์ไป... ได้ไหม

Can you please clean my room?

gà-rú-naa tam-kwaam-sà-àat hôong dûuai dâi măi

กรุณาทำความสะอาดห้องด้วยได้ไหม

I'd like room service.

chăn/pŏm yàak sàng aa-hăan maa taan nai hôong

ฉัน/ผม อยากสั่งอาหารมาทานในห้อง

Can you please wake me up at...?

gà-rú-naa bplùk chăn/pŏm wee-laa...dâi măi

กรุณาปลุก ฉัน/ผม เวลา...ได้ไหม

Can I pay with a credit card?

chăn/pŏm jàai dûuai bàt kree-dit dâi măi

ฉัน/ผม จ่ายด้วยบัตรเครดิตได้ไหม

Okay, I'll take it.

dtòk-long chăn/pŏm ao hôong níi

ตกลง ฉัน/ผม เอาห้องนี้

I'd like a room with a garden view.

chăn/pŏm yàak dâi hôong tîi moong hĕn sŭuan

ฉัน/ผม อยากได้ห้องที่มองเห็นสวน

Looking for Lodging

I'd like a room with an ocean view.   chăn/pŏm yàak dâi hôong tîi moong hĕn tá-lee

ฉัน/ผม อยากได้ห้องที่มองเห็นทะเล

There's a problem with my...   ...mii bpan-hăa

...มีปัญหา

- ...shower (electric shower).   fàk-bua

  ฝักบัว

- ...toilet / bathroom.   hôong nám

  ห้องน้ำ

- ...sink.   àang-láang-muu

  อ่างล้างมือ

- ...drain.   tôo rá-baai nám

  ท่อระบายน้ำ

- ...TV.   too-rá-tát

  โทรทัศน์

- ...air conditioner.   krûuang bpràp-aa-gàat

  เครื่องปรับอากาศ

- ...fan.   pát-lom

  พัดลม

- ...window.   nâa-dtàang

  หน้าต่าง

- ...bedroom.   hôong-noon

  ห้องนอน

- ...room.   hôong

  ห้อง

12. Where Am I Going...and How Do I Get There?

12.1 Getting Around Thailand

Where can I buy a ... ticket?	chǎn/pǒm sǎa-mâat súɯ dtǔua... dâi tîi-nǎi
	ฉัน/ผม สามารถซื้อตั๋ว...ได้ที่ไหน
• ...train...	rót-fai
	รถไฟ
• ...bus...	rót dooi-sǎan
	รถโดยสาร
• ...ferry...	rɯɯa-kâam-fâak
	เรือข้ามฟาก
• ...plane...	krɯ̂ɯang-bin
	เครื่องบิน
Train Station	sà-tǎa-nii rót-fai
	สถานีรถไฟ
Bus Station	sà-tǎa-nii kǒn-sòng
	สถานีขนส่ง
Ferry Terminal	sà-tǎa-nii rɯɯa-kâam-fâak
	สถานีเรือข้ามฟาก
Airport	sà-nǎam-bin
	สนามบิน
• Suvarnabumi	Sù-wan-ná-puum
	สุวรรณภูมิ
• Don Mueang	Dɔɔn Mɯɯang
	ดอนเมือง

Where Am I Going...and How Do I Get There?

Ticket Window	chɔ̂ɔng súu dtǔua ช่องซื้อตั๋ว
Travel Agent	bɔɔ-rí-sàt tôong-tîiao บริษัทท่องเที่ยว
Does this bus go to....?	rót dooi-sǎan kan níi bpai...châi mǎi รถโดยสารคันนี้ไป…ใช่ไหม
Does this train go to....?	rót-fai kà-buuan níi bpai...châi mǎi รถไฟขบวนนี้ไป…ใช่ไหม
Does this bus stop at...?	rót dooi-sǎan kan níi jɔ̀ɔt tîi... châi mǎi รถโดยสารคันนี้จอดที่…ใช่ไหม
Does this train stop at...?	rót-fai kà-buuan níi jɔ̀ɔt tîi... châi mǎi รถไฟขบวนนี้จอดที่…ใช่ไหม
When will this bus arrive?	rót dooi-sǎan kan níi jà maa tǔng mûua-rai รถโดยสารคันนี้จะมาถึงเมื่อไร
When will this train arrive?	rót-fai kà-buuan níi jà maa tǔng mûua-rai รถไฟขบวนนี้จะมาถึงเมื่อไร
When will this bus depart?	rót dooi-sǎan kan níi jà ɔ̀ɔk mûua-rai รถโดยสารคันนี้จะออกเมื่อไร
When will this train depart?	rót-fai kà-buuan níi jà ɔ̀ɔk mûua-rai รถไฟขบวนนี้จะออกเมื่อไร
What time does the first bus depart?	rót dooi-sǎan ɔ̀ɔk kan rɛ̂ɛk gìi moong รถโดยสารออกคันแรก กี่โมง

What time does the first train depart?	rót-fai ɔ̀ɔk kà-buuan rɛ̂ɛk gìi moong
	รถไฟออกขบวนแรก กี่โมง
What time does the last bus depart?	rót dooi-sǎan ɔ̀ɔk kan sùt-táai gìi moong
	รถโดยสารออกคันสุดท้าย กี่โมง
What time does the last train depart?	rót-fai ɔ̀ɔk kà-buuan sùt-táai gìi moong
	รถไฟออกขบวนสุดท้าย กี่โมง
What station is this?	nîi kɯɯ sà-tǎa-nii à-rai
	นี่คือสถานีอะไร
I need a one-way (single) ticket to...	chǎn/pǒm dtɔ̂ɔng-gaan dtǔua tîiao-diiao bpai...
	ฉัน/ผม ต้องการตั๋วเที่ยวเดียว ไป...
I need a round-trip (return) ticket to...	chǎn/pǒm dtɔ̂ɔng-gaan dtǔua bpai-glàp bpai
	ฉัน/ผม ต้องการตั๋วไป-กลับ ไป...
I would like a...	chǎn/pǒm yàak dâi...nɯ̀ng tîi
	ฉัน/ผม อยากได้...หนึ่งที่
• ...1st class sleeping car.	rót nɔɔn chán-nɯ̀ng
	รถนอนชั้นหนึ่ง
• ...2nd class sleeping car.	rót nɔɔn chán sɔ̌ɔng
	รถนอนชั้นสอง
• ...1st class seat.	tîi-nâng chán-nɯ̀ng
	ที่นั่งชั้นหนึ่ง

Where Am I Going...and How Do I Get There?

- ...2nd class seat.
tîi-nâng chán-sɔ̌ɔng
ที่นั่งชั้นสอง

- ...3rd class seat.
tîi-nâng chán-sǎam
ที่นั่งชั้นสาม

Is there a fan?
mii pát-lom mǎi
มีพัดลมไหม

Is the bus air-conditioned?
rót dooi-sǎan kan níi bpràp aa-gàat mǎi
รถโดยสารคันนี้ปรับอากาศไหม

Is the train air-conditioned?
rót-fai kà-buuan níi bràp aa-gàat mǎi
รถไฟขบวนนี้ปรับอากาศไหม

Is there a restaurant car on the train?
mii ráan aa-hǎan bon rót-fai kà-buuan níi mǎi
มีร้านอาหารบนรถไฟขบวนนี้ไหม

I want to leave…
chǎn/pǒm dtɔ̂ɔng-gaan dəən-taang…
ฉัน/ผม ต้องการเดินทาง...

- ...today.
wan-níi
วันนี้

- ...tomorrow.
wan prûng-níi
วันพรุ่งนี้

- ...next week.
sàp-daa nâa
สัปดาห์หน้า

How long does it take to get to...?
bpai...chái wee-laa naan kɛ̂ɛ nǎi
ไป...ใช้เวลานานแค่ไหน

Is there an earlier bus?
mii rót dooi-sǎan tîi ɔ̀ɔk reo gwàa níi mǎi
มีรถโดยสารที่ออกเร็วกว่านี้ไหม

Is there a later bus?	mii rót dooi-sǎan tîi ɔ̀ɔk cháa gwàa níi mǎi
	มีรถโดยสารที่ออกช้ากว่านี้ไหม
Is there an earlier train?	mii rót-fai tîi ɔ̀ɔk reo gwàa níi mǎi
	มีรถไฟที่ออกเร็วกว่านี้ไหม
Is there a later train?	mii rót-fai tîi ɔ̀ɔk cháa gwàa níi mǎi
	มีรถไฟที่ออกช้ากว่านี้ไหม
I'd like to reserve a seat.	chǎn/pǒm yàak jɔɔng tîi-nâng
	ฉัน/ผม อยากจองที่นั่ง
I'd like a window seat.	chǎn/pǒm yàak dâi tîi-nâng dtìt nǎa-dtàang
	ฉัน/ผม อยากได้ที่นั่งติดหน้าต่าง
I'd like an aisle seat.	chǎn/pǒm yàak dâi tîi-nâng dtìt taang-dəən
	ฉัน/ผม อยากได้ที่นั่งติดทางเดิน
Do I need to change trains?	chǎn/pǒm dtɔ̂ɔng bplìian rót-fai mǎi
	ฉัน/ผม ต้องเปลี่ยนรถไฟไหม
Where can I leave my luggage?	chǎn/pǒm sǎa-mâat gèp grà-bpǎo-dəən-taang wái tîi-nǎi dâi
	ฉัน/ผม สามารถเก็บกระเป๋าเดินทางไว้ที่ไหนได้
Is this ticket refundable?	dtǔua bai níi kʉʉn ngəən dâi mǎi
	ตั๋วใบนี้คืนเงินได้ไหม
Is this seat taken?	tîi nâng níi tùuk jɔɔng rʉ̌ʉ yang
	ที่นั่งนี้ถูกจองหรือยัง

12.2 Getting Around Town

12.2.1 Directions

Go straight.	dtrong bpai
	ตรงไป

Where Am I Going...and How Do I Get There?

Turn left.	líiao sáai เลี้ยวซ้าย
Turn right.	líiao kwǎa เลี้ยวขวา
Keep left.	yùu sáai อยู่ซ้าย
Keep right.	yùu kwǎa อยู่ขวา
Stop here.	yùt tîi-nîi หยุดที่นี่
Stop there on the left.	yùt tîi-nân dâan sáai หยุดที่นั่นด้านซ้าย
Stop there on the right.	yùt tîi-nân dâan kwǎa หยุดที่นั่นด้านขวา
Stop in front of…	yùt dâan nâa… หยุดด้านหน้า…

- …7/11. see-wêen ii-lee-wêen เซเว่น อีเลเว่น
- …the hotel. roong-rɛɛm โรงแรม
- …the station. sà-tǎa-nii สถานี
- …the traffic lights. fai jà-raa-jɔɔn ไฟจราจร

Stop behind the… yùt dâan lǎng…
หยุดด้านหลัง…

- ...car.
  rót-yon
  รถยนต์

- ...truck.
  rót ban-túk
  รถบรรทุก

- ...bus.
  rót dooi-săan
  รถโดยสาร

- ...motorcycle.
  mɔɔ-dtêə-sai
  มอเตอร์ไซค์

Don't stop here.
yàa yùt tîi-nîi
อย่าหยุดที่นี่

Stop in 100m.
ìik nùng rɔ́ɔi méet lɛ́ɛo yùt
อีกหนึ่งร้อยเมตรแล้วหยุด

12.2.2 With a Driver

Where can I find a...
chăn/pŏm săa-mâat hăa...dâi tîi năi
ฉัน/ผม สามารถหา...ได้ที่ไหน

- ...taxi.
  rót tɛ́k-sîi
  รถแท็กซี่

- ...tuk-tuk.
  rót túk-túk
  รถตุ๊กตุ๊ก

- ...red truck (slow taxi).
  rót sɔ̌ɔng-tɛ̌ɛo
  รถสองแถว

Can you take me to...?
kun chûuai paa chăn/pŏm bpai... dâi măi
คุณช่วยพา ฉัน/ผม ไป...ได้ไหม

How much to go to...?
bpai... tâo-rai
ไป... เท่าไร

Where Am I Going...and How Do I Get There?

(If the price is exorbitant) Hahaha, no, really. How much?
(don't forget to smile :-)

mâi *[pause for emphasis]* jing-jing tâo-rai

ไม่ *[pause]* จริงๆ เท่าไร

Can you please tell me when we get there?

gà-rú-naa bɔ̀ɔk chǎn/pǒm mûea bpai tǔng tîi-nân dâi mǎi

กรุณาบอก ฉัน/ผม เมื่อไปถึงที่นั่นได้ไหม

Can you call a taxi for me please?

gà-rú-naa rîiak tɛ́k-sii hâi chǎn/pǒm nɔ̀ɔi dâi mǎi

กรุณาเรียกแท๊กซี่ให้ ฉัน/ผม หน่อยได้ไหม

Can you pick me up tomorrow at my hotel please?

gà-rú-naa maa ráp chǎn/pǒm wan prûng-níi tîi roong-rɛɛm dâi mǎi

กรุณามารับ ฉัน/ผม วันพรุ่งนี้ที่โรงแรม ได้ไหม

Do you know where... is?

kun rúu mǎi wâa... yùu tîi-nǎi

คุณรู้ไหมว่า... อยู่ที่ไหน

I know how to get there.

chǎn/pǒm rúu taang bpai tîi-nân

ฉัน/ผม รู้ทางไปที่นั่น

How much would you charge to drive us around for... hours?

paa pûuak-rao bpai rɔ̂ɔp-rɔ̂ɔp bprà-maan... chûua-moong kun kít tâo-rai

พาพวกเราไปรอบๆ ประมาณ ...ชั่วโมง คุณคิดเท่าไร

Can you wait here for me?

gà-rú-naa rɔɔ chǎn/pǒm tîi-nîi dâi mǎi

กรุณารอ ฉัน/ผม ที่นี่ได้ไหม

Can you come back in.... hour(s)?	gà-rú-naa glàp maa ìik ... chûua-moong dâi măi
	กรุณากลับมาอีก ... ชั่วโมง ได้ไหม

12.2.3 Want Your Own Transport?

I want to rent a...	chǎn/pǒm dtôɔng-gaan châo...
	ฉัน/ผม ต้องการเช่า...
• ...motorcycle.	mɔɔ-dtêə-sai
	มอเตอร์ไซค์
• ...car.	rót-yon
	รถยนต์
• ...bicycle.	jàk-grà-yaan
	จักรยาน
Can I park here?	chǎn/pǒm jɔ̀ɔt rót tîi-nîi dâi mǎi
	ฉัน/ผม จอดรถที่นี่ได้ไหม
Where can I park?	chǎn/pǒm sǎa-mâat jɔ̀ɔt rót dâi tîi-nǎi
	ฉัน/ผม สามารถจอดรถได้ที่ไหน
I got a ticket. Where can I pay it?	chǎn/pǒm dâi bai-sàng. chǎn/pǒm sǎa-mâat bpai sǐia kâa bpràp dâi tîi-nǎi
	ฉัน/ผม ได้ใบสั่ง
	ฉัน/ผม สามารถไปเสียค่าปรับได้ที่ไหน
Fill the tank.	dtəəm dtem tăng
	เติมเต็มถัง
Put in... baht.	dtəəm...baat
	เติม...บาท

Where Am I Going...and How Do I Get There?

- ...100...   nùng rɔ́ɔi
- ...200...   sɔ̌ɔng rɔ́ɔi
- ...300...   sǎam rɔ́ɔi
- ...400...   sìi rɔ́ɔi
- ...500...   hâa rɔ́ɔi

Where can I find a good...?   chǎn/pǒm sǎa-mâat hǎa... dii-dii dâi tîi-nǎi

ฉัน/ผม สามารถหา... ดีๆ ได้ที่ไหน

- ...restaurant.   ráan aa-hǎan

  ร้านอาหาร

- ...hotel.   roong-rɛɛm

  โรงแรม

- ...market.   dtà-làat

  ตลาด

- ...beach.   hàat

  หาด

Where's the nearest...?   ...tîi glâi tîi sùt yùu tîi-nǎi

...ที่ใกล้ที่สุด อยู่ที่ไหน

- ...drug store (pharmacy).   ráan kǎai-yaa

  ร้านขายยา

- ...bank.   tá-naa-kaan

  ธนาคาร

- ...police station.   sà-tǎa-nii dtam-rùat

  สถานีตำรวจ

- ...gas station.   bpám nám-man

  ปั๊มน้ำมัน

- …fish restaurant. ráan aa-hăan tîi mii bplaa
  ร้านอาหารที่มีปลา

- …Chinese restaurant. ráan aa-hăan jiin
  ร้านอาหารจีน

- …Indian restaurant. ráan aa-hăan in-diia
  ร้านอาหารอินเดีย

- …Mexican restaurant. ráan aa-hăan mék-sí-gan
  ร้านอาหารเม็กซิกัน

- …Malaysian restaurant. ráan aa-hăan maa-lay-siia
  ร้านอาหารมาเลเซีย

- …Turkish restaurant. ráan aa-hăan dtù-rá-gii
  ร้านอาหารตุรกี

- …museum. pí-pít-tá-pan
  พิพิธภัณฑ์

- …post office. bprai-sà-nii
  ไปรษณีย์

- …church. bòot
  โบสถ์

- …mosque. sù-rào
  สุเหร่า

- …temple. wát
  วัด

- …supermarket. súu-bpəə-maa-gèt
  ซูเปอร์มาร์เก็ต

- …bar. baa
  บาร์

- …BTS Station. sà-tăa-nii bii-tii-éet
  สถานีบีทีเอส
- …MRT Station (Bangkok Underground). sà-tăa-nii rót-fai-fáa tâi-din
  สถานีรถไฟฟ้าใต้ดิน

13. Culinary Considerations

Can you recommend a good restaurant? kun chûuai nέε nam ráan aa-hăan dii-dii hâi nòoi dâi măi
คุณช่วยแนะนำร้านอาหารดีๆ ให้หน่อยได้ไหม

I like spicy food. chăn/pŏm chôop taan aa-hăan pèt
ฉัน/ผม ชอบทานอาหารเผ็ด

I can't eat spicy food. chăn/pŏm mâi taan aa-hăan pèt
ฉัน/ผม ไม่ทานอาหารเผ็ด

This is delicious. níi à-ròoi mâak
นี่ อร่อยมาก

I'm a vegetarian. chăn/pŏm gin-jee
ฉัน/ผม กินเจ

I like… chăn/pŏm chôop…
ฉัน/ผม ชอบ…

I don't like… chăn/pŏm mâi chôop…
ฉัน/ผม ไม่ชอบ…

Please add… gà-rú-naa sài…
กรุณาใส่…

Please don't add...	gà-rú-naa yàa sài... กรุณาอย่าใส่...
• ...pork.	núa mǔu เนื้อหมู
• ...chicken.	núa gài เนื้อไก่
• ...beef.	núa wuua เนื้อวัว
• ...blood.	lûat เลือด
• ...vegetables.	pàk ผัก
• ...viscera.	krûang-nai เครื่องใน
• ...a fried egg.	kài-daao ไข่ดาว
Do you have an English menu?	kun mii raai-gaan aa-hǎan bpen paa-sǎa ang-grìt mǎi คุณมีรายการอาหารเป็นภาษาอังกฤษไหม
Do you have western food?	kun mii aa-hǎan fà-ràng mǎi คุณมีอาหารฝรั่งไหม
What's your favourite Thai dish?	aa-hǎan tai tîi kun chɔ̂ɔp kɯɯ à-rai อาหารไทยที่คุณชอบคืออะไร
What's in that?	nân sài à-rai bâang นั่น ใส่อะไรบ้าง

Culinary Considerations

I'd like something with...	chǎn/pǒm yàak dâi...gàp à-rai gɔ̂ dâi

ฉัน/ผม อยากได้...กับอะไรก็ได้

- ...rice. kâao sǔuai

  ข้าวสวย

- ...noodles. gǔuai-dtǐiao

  ก๋วยเตี๋ยว

I'd like a table for... people. chǎn/pǒm yàak dâi dtó sǎm-ràp ... kon

ฉัน/ผม อยากได้โต๊ะสำหรับ...คน

I'd like the bill please. gèp ngəən dûuai

เก็บเงินด้วย

What is this charge for? nîi kâa à-rai

นี่ค่าอะไร

Is there a VAT and service fee included? ruuam paa-sǐi lɛ́ɛ kâa bɔɔ-rí-gaan lɛ́ɛo châi mǎi

รวมภาษีและค่าบริการแล้วใช่ไหม

I'm allergic to... chǎn/pǒm pɛ́ɛ...

ฉัน/ผม แพ้...

- ...wheat (gluten). kâao sǎa-lii

  ข้าวสาลี

- ...nuts. tùua

  ถั่ว

- ...seafood. aa-hǎan tà-lee

  อาหารทะเล

- ...shellfish. sàt-nám bprà-pêet mii bplùuak

  สัตว์น้ำประเภทมีเปลือก

I'd like a hot drink.	chăn/pŏm yàak dâi krûuang dùum rɔ́ɔn-rɔ́ɔn
	ฉัน/ผม อยากได้เครื่องดื่มร้อนๆ
I'd like a cold drink.	chăn/pŏm yàak dâi krûuang dùum yen-yen
	ฉัน/ผม อยากได้เครื่องดื่มเย็นๆ
What are they eating?	pûuak-kăo gam-lang gin à-rai
	พวกเขากำลังกินอะไร
I'd like to try that.	chăn/pŏm yàak lɔɔng taan bɛ̀ɛp nán
	ฉัน/ผม อยากลองทานแบบนั้น
What is a local specialty?	aa-hăan tîi mii chûu kɔ̌ɔng tîi-nîi kuu à-rai
	อาหารที่มีชื่อของที่นี่คืออะไร
Where can I find it?	chăn/pŏm săa-mâat hăa dâi tîi-năi
	ฉัน/ผม สามารถหาได้ที่ไหน
What is this?	nîi kuu à-rai
	นี่คืออะไร
What is that?	nán kuu à-rai
	นั่นคืออะไร
Is it spicy?	pèt măi
	เผ็ดไหม
What is it made of?	man tam maa jàak à-rai
	มันทำมาจากอะไร
Can I try a small taste?	kɔ̌ɔ lɔɔng chim nɔ̀ɔi dâi măi
	ขอลองชิมหน่อยได้ไหม
How do I eat this?	nîi taan yang ngai
	นี่ทานยังไง

Culinary Considerations

Excuse me (to get the server's attention).	kɔ̌ɔ-tôot
	ขอโทษ
• (If the waiter looks or is younger than you)	nɔ́ɔng
	น้อง
• (If the waiter looks or is older than you)	pîi
	พี่
Am I allowed to smoke here?	tîi-nîi sùup bù-rìi dâi măi
	ที่นี่สูบบุหรี่ได้ไหม

14. Feeling a Little Parched

I'd like a bottle of…	chăn/pŏm yàak dâi … nùng kùuat
	ฉัน/ผม อยากได้…หนึ่งขวด
I'd like a glass of …	chăn/pŏm yàak dâi … nùng gɛ̂ɛo
	ฉัน/ผม อยากได้…หนึ่งแก้ว
I'd like a cup of …	chăn/pŏm yàak dâi … nùng tûuai
	ฉัน/ผม อยากได้…หนึ่งถ้วย
• …Pepsi / Sprite / Fanta.	bpéep-sîi / sà-prai / fɛɛn-dtâa
	เป๊ปซี่ / สไปรท์ / แฟนต้า
• …water.	nám bplào
	น้ำเปล่า
• …coffee/ tea / chocolate / Ovaltine.	gaa-fɛɛ / chaa /
	chɔ́k-goo-lɛ́t / oo-wan-tin
	กาแฟ / ชา / ช็อกโกแลต / โอวัลติน
• Another round, please.	kɔ̌ɔ iik nùng
	ขออีกหนึ่ง

English	Thai (romanized)
I'd like a fruit smoothie, please.	chăn/pŏm yàak dâi nám pŏn-lá-mái bpàn nùng gɛ̂ɛo

ฉัน/ผม อยากได้น้ำผลไม้ปั่น หนึ่งแก้ว

Do you serve alcohol?	kun kăai krûuang-dùum ɛɛ-gɔɔ-hɔɔ măi

คุณขายเครื่องดื่มแอลกอฮอล์ไหม

I'd like a bottle of …	chăn/pŏm yàak dâi... nùng kùuat

ฉัน/ผม อยากได้...หนึ่งขวด

I'd like a glass of …	chăn/pŏm yàak dâi... nùng gɛ̂ɛo

ฉัน/ผม อยากได้...หนึ่งแก้ว

- …Thai beer. — biia tai

  เบียร์ไทย

- …imported beer. — biia nɔ̂ɔk

  เบียร์นอก

- …whiskey. — wít-sà-gîi

  วิสกี้

- …red / white wine. — wai dɛɛng / wai kăao

  ไวน์แดง / ไวน์ขาว

Cheers ('bottoms-up')!	chai-yoo

ไชโย

Please add...	gà-rú-naa sài

กรุณาใส่

Please don't add...	gà-rú-naa yàa sài

กรุณาอย่าใส่

- …salt. — gluua

  เกลือ

- ...sugar.　　　　　　　　　　　　　　　　nám dtaan
　　　　　　　　　　　　　　　　　　　　　น้ำตาล

- ...syrup.　　　　　　　　　　　　　　　　nám chûuam
　　　　　　　　　　　　　　　　　　　　　น้ำเชื่อม

- ...milk.　　　　　　　　　　　　　　　　　nom
　　　　　　　　　　　　　　　　　　　　　นม

- ...condensed milk.　　　　　　　　　　　nóm kôn
　　　　　　　　　　　　　　　　　　　　　นมข้น

- ...ice.　　　　　　　　　　　　　　　　　nám kěng
　　　　　　　　　　　　　　　　　　　　　น้ำแข็ง

15. Seeking Souvenirs

How much is this?　　　　　　　　　　　nîi raa-kaa tâo-rai
　　　　　　　　　　　　　　　　　　　　นี่ราคาเท่าไร

How much is that?　　　　　　　　　　　nân raa-kaa tâo-rai
　　　　　　　　　　　　　　　　　　　　นั่นราคาเท่าไร

Do you sell...?　　　　　　　　　　　　　kun kǎai...mǎi
　　　　　　　　　　　　　　　　　　　　คุณขาย...ไหม

I'd like to buy...　　　　　　　　　　　　chǎn/pǒm yàak súu...
　　　　　　　　　　　　　　　　　　　　ฉัน/ผม อยากซื้อ...

That's a good price. I will take this / that.　　　raa-kaa mâi pɛɛng.
　　　　　　　　　　　chǎn/pǒm jà ao an-níi / an-nán
　ราคาไม่แพง ฉัน/ผม จะเอาอันนี้ / อันนั้น

Do you like it?　　　　　　　　　　　　kun chɔ̂ɔp mǎi
　　　　　　　　　　　　　　　　　　　　คุณชอบไหม

I really like it.	chăn/pŏm chɔ̂ɔp mâak	ฉัน/ผม ชอบมาก
Really?	jing-rǎɘ	จริงเหรอ
Really!	jing-jing	จริงๆ
Look!	duu nân sì	ดูนั่นสิ
Hurry up.	réo-réo	เร็วๆ
That's expensive.	pɛɛng	แพง
That is not expensive.	măi pɛɛng	ไม่แพง
Can you give me a discount?	kun chûuai lót hâi chăn/pŏm nɔ̀ɔi dâi măi	คุณช่วยลดให้ ฉัน/ผม หน่อยได้ไหม
What if I buy more than one?	lɛ́ɛo tâa chăn/pŏm súɯ mâak gwàa nɯ̀ng là	แล้วถ้า ฉัน/ผม ซื้อมากกว่าหนึ่งหล่ะ
Do you have a bigger size?	kun mii kà-nàat yàai gwàa níi măi	คุณมีขนาดใหญ่กว่านี้ไหม
Do you have a smaller size?	kun mii kà-nàat lék gwàa níi măi	คุณมีขนาดเล็กกว่านี้ไหม
Do you have this in a different colour?	kun mii sǐi ɯ̀ɯn bɛ̀ɛp níi măi	คุณมีสีอื่นแบบนี้ไหม

Seeking Souvenirs

No, thank you. I already have one of those. mái *[pause]* kɔ̌ɔp kun chǎn/pǒm mii bɛ̀ɛp nán lɛ́ɛo
ไม่ *[pause]* ขอบคุณ ฉัน/ผม มีแบบนั้นแล้ว

It's not exactly what I'm looking for. man mâi châi sìng tîi chǎn/pǒm gam-lang mɔɔng hǎa yùu
มันไม่ใช่สิ่งที่ ฉัน/ผม กำลังมองหาอยู่

Do you ship overseas? kun sòng bpai dtàang bprà-têet mǎi
คุณส่งไปต่างประเทศไหม

Do you have a certificate of authenticity? kun mii bai ráp-rɔɔng sǐn-káa hâi mǎi
คุณมีใบรับรองสินค้าให้ไหม

Is this... nîi kɯɯ ... châi mǎi
นี่คือ...ใช่ไหม

- ...silk? pâa mǎi
  ผ้าไหม

- ...cotton? pâa fâai
  ผ้าฝ้าย

- ...antique? kɔ̌ɔng boo-raan
  ของโบราณ

- ...authentic? kɔ̌ɔng tɛ́ɛ
  ของแท้

- ...made in Thailand? kɔ̌ɔng tîi tam nai mɯɯang tai
  ของที่ทำในเมืองไทย

Where can I find...? chǎn/pǒm sǎa-mâat hǎa ... dâi tîi-nǎi
ฉัน/ผม สามารถหา...ได้ที่ไหน

Can I have a bag?	chăn/pŏm kɔ̌ɔ tŭng dâi măi
	ฉัน/ผม ขอถุงได้ไหม
I don't need a bag?	chăn/pŏm mâi ao tŭng
	ฉัน/ผม ไม่เอาถุง
Do you have a business card?	kun mii naam-bàt măi
	คุณมีนามบัตรไหม
Are you open tomorrow?	wan prûng-níi kun bpə̀ət măi
	วันพรุ่งนี้คุณเปิดไหม
Will you be here tomorrow?	wan prûng-níi kun jà yùu tîi-nîi măi
	วันพรุ่งนี้คุณจะอยู่ที่นี่ไหม
What time do you open?	kun bpə̀ət gìi moong
	คุณเปิดกี่โมง
What time do you close?	kun bpìt gìi moong
	คุณปิดกี่โมง

16. I Should Have Brought More Money

Where is the nearest ...	... tîi glâi tîi sùt yùu tîi-năi
	...ที่ใกล้ที่สุด อยู่ที่ไหน
• ...bank?	tá-naa-kaan
	ธนาคาร
• ...ATM?	dtûu ee-tii-em
	ตู้เอทีเอ็ม
• ...currency exchange?	tîi lɛ̂ɛk bpliian ngəən-dtraa
	ที่แลกเปลี่ยนเงินตรา

I Should Have Brought More Money

I need to exchange... into Thai Baht.
chăn/pŏm dtôong-gaan lɛ̂ɛk ... bpen ngəən baat tai
ฉัน/ผม ต้องการแลก...เป็นเงินบาทไทย

- ...dollars...
ngəən don-lâa
เงินดอลลาร์

- ...yen...
ngəən yeen
เงินเยน

- ...euros...
ngəən yuu-roo
เงินยูโร

- ...pounds...
ngəən bpɔɔn
เงินปอนด์

Can I exchange traveler's cheques (checks) here?
chăn/pŏm săa-mâat lɛ̂ɛk chék dəən-taang tîi-nîi dâi măi
ฉัน/ผม สามารถแลกเช็คเดินทางที่นี่ได้ไหม

What is the exchange rate?
àt-dtraa lɛ̂ɛk bpliian tâo-rai
อัตราแลกเปลี่ยนเท่าไร

I'd like small notes, please.
chăn/pŏm yàak dâi bɛɛng yɔ̂ɔi
ฉัน/ผม อยากได้แบงค์ย่อย

I'd like large notes, please.
chăn/pŏm yàak dâi bɛɛng yài
ฉัน/ผม อยากได้แบงค์ใหญ่

17. I Have a Question...

Who?
krai
ใคร

What?
à-rai
อะไร

When?	mûua-rai
	เมื่อไร
Where?	tîi-năi
	ที่ไหน
Why?	tam-mai
	ทำไม
How much / how many	tâo-rai
	เท่าไร
How often?	bɔ̀ɔi kɛ̂ɛ năi
	บ่อยแค่ไหน
Is... possible?	...bpen bpai dâi măi
	... เป็นไปได้ไหม
Is... okay?	...dtók-long măi
	...ตกลงไหม
Is... right?	...tùuk dtɔ̂ɔng măi
	...ถูกต้องไหม
Do you have....?	kun mii...măi
	คุณมี...ไหม

18. Emergencies

Help!	chûuai dûuai
	ช่วยด้วย
I lost my...	...kɔ̌ɔng chǎn/pǒm hǎai
	...ของ ฉัน/ผม หาย

- ...bag.   grà-bpǎo
  กระเป๋า
- ...passport.   nǎng-sʉ̌ʉ dəən-taang
  หนังสือเดินทาง
- ...tickets.   dtǔua
  ตั๋ว
- ...room key.   gun-jɛɛ hɔ̌ɔng
  กุญแจห้อง
- ...wallet.   grà-bpǎo-ngəən
  กระเป๋าเงิน

I need to see a doctor.   chǎn/pǒm dtɔ̂ɔng-gaan póp mɔ̌ɔ
ฉัน/ผม ต้องการพบหมอ

I need to see a dentist.   chǎn/pǒm dtɔ̂ɔng-gaan póp mɔ̌ɔ-fan
ฉัน/ผม ต้องการพบหมอฟัน

I feel sick.   chǎn/pǒm rúu-sùk mâi sà-baai
ฉัน/ผม รู้สึกไม่สบาย

I need the police.   chǎn/pǒm dtɔ̂ɔng-gaan póp dtam-ruuat
ฉัน/ผม ต้องการพบตำรวจ

English	Thai (romanized)
I need the tourist police.	chăn/pŏm dtôong-gaan póp dtam-ruuat tôong-tîiao

ฉัน/ผม ต้องการพบตำรวจท่องเที่ยว

Can I borrow your phone?	chăn/pŏm kŏo yuum too-rá-sàp kŏong kun dâi măi

ฉัน/ผม ขอยืมโทรศัพท์ของคุณได้ไหม

Please call the police.	gà-rú-naa too rîiak dtam-rùuat

กรุณาโทรเรียกตำรวจ

I've had an accident.	chăn/pŏm dâi ráp u-bàt-hèet

ฉัน/ผม ได้รับอุบัติเหตุ

I need to contact the... embassy.	chăn/pŏm dtôong-gaan dtìt-dtòo gàp sà-tăan tûut...

ฉัน/ผม ต้องการติดต่อกับสถานทูต...

I need to contact the... consulate.	chăn/pŏm dtôong-gaan dtìt-dtòo gàp sà-tăan gong-sŭn...

ฉันผม/ ต้องการติดต่อกับสถานกงสุล...

- ...American... — ə-mee-rí-gan

  อเมริกา

- ...British... — ang-grít

  อังกฤษ

- ...Australian... — òot-sà-dtree-liia

  ออสเตรเลีย

- ...Canadian... — kɛɛ-naa-daa

  แคนาดา

- ...New Zealand... — nio-sii-lɛɛn

  นิวซีแลนด์

Emergencies

- ...South African... ɛ̀ɛp-frí-gaa dtâi
  แอฟริกาใต้

Natural Disasters

Natural Disasters pai tam-má-châat
ภัยธรรมชาติ

- flood nám-tûuam
  น้ำท่วม

- earthquake pɛ̀ɛn-din-wăi
  แผ่นดินไหว

- tsunami sù-naa-mí
  สึนามิ

Am I being arrested? chăn/pŏm gam-lang tùuk jàp châi măi
ฉัน/ผม กำลังถูกจับใช่ไหม

I want a lawyer. chăn/pŏm dtɔ̂ɔng-gaan tá-naai
ฉัน/ผม ต้องการทนาย

I need a translator. chăn/pŏm dtɔ̂ɔng-gaan lâam
ฉัน/ผม ต้องการล่าม

18.1 In Case of a Little Emergency (At the Pharmacy)

Pharmacy (drug store / chemist) ráan kăai-yaa
ร้านขายยา

I have (a)... chăn/pŏm...
ฉัน/ผม...

- ...headache. bpùuat hŭua
  ปวดหัว

- ...stomach ache.   bpùuat tɔ́ɔng
  ปวดท้อง
- ...diarrhoea.   tɔ́ɔng-rûuang
  ท้องร่วง
- ...blister.   bpen pǐo-nǎng pú-pɔɔng
  เป็นผิวหนังพุพอง
- ...sunburn.   tùuk sɛ̌ɛng-dɛ̀ɛt jon pǐo-nǎng àk-sèep
  ถูกแสงแดดจนผิวหนังอักเสบ
- ...cold.   bpen kâi-wàt
  เป็นไข้หวัด
- ...rash.   bpen pɯ̀ɯn bon pǐo-nǎng
  เป็นผื่นบนผิวหนัง

Do you carry...   kun mii...mǎi
คุณมี...ไหม

- ...Tylenol?   tai-lí-nɔɔn
  ไทลินอล
- ...Aspirin?   ɛ́ɛt-sà-pai-rin
  แอสไพริน
- ...sunscreen?   kriim gan-dɛ̀ɛt
  ครีมกันแดด
- ...tiger balm?   yaa-mɔ̀ɔng
  ยาหม่อง
- ...Imodium?   i-moo-diiam
  อิโมเดียม
- ...band-aids?   pláat-sà-dtə̂ə
  พลาสเตอร์

Emergencies

- ...toothpaste? yaa-sǐi-fan
  ยาสีฟัน
- ...deodorant? lûuk-glîng
  ลูกกลิ้ง
- ...feminine hygiene products? pà-lìt-dtà-pan tam kwaam sà-àat sǎm-ràp pûu-yǐng
  ผลิตภัณฑ์ทำความสะอาดสำหรับผู้หญิง
- ...condoms? tǔng yaang a-naa-mai
  ถุงยางอนามัย

19. The Kids Are Alright

I am traveling with my family.   chǎn/pǒm dəən-taang gàp krɔ̂ɔp-kruua
ฉัน/ผม เดินทางกับครอบครัว

I have... daughters.   chǎn/pǒm mii lûuk-sǎao...kon
ฉัน/ผม มีลูกสาว...คน

I have... sons.   chǎn/pǒm mii lûuk-chaai ...kon
ฉัน/ผม มีลูกชาย...คน

She is... years old.   lûuk-sǎao aa-yú ...bpii
ลูกสาวอายุ...ปี

He is... years old.   lûuk-chaai aa-yú ...bpii
ลูกชายอายุ...ปี

Where can I buy...   chǎn/pǒm sǎa-mâat súɯ ...dâi tîi-nǎi
ฉัน/ผม สามารถซื้อ...ได้ที่ไหน

- ...bottles?

  kùuat nom

  ขวดนม

- ...diapers?

  pâa ɔ̂ɔm

  ผ้าอ้อม

- ...baby wipes?

  grà-dàat chét gôn dèk taa-rók

  กระดาษเช็ดก้นเด็กทารก

- ...sunscreen?

  kriim gan-dɛ̀ɛt

  ครีมกันแดด

- ...baby formula?

  aa-hǎan dèk-taa-rók

  อาหารเด็กทารก

Do you have a...

kun mii...mǎi

คุณมี...ไหม

- ...crib?

  dtiiang-nɔɔn dèk

  เตียงนอนเด็ก

- ... stroller?

  rót-kěn sài dèk

  รถเข็นใส่เด็ก

- ... car seat?

  tîi-nâng dèk nai rót-yon

  ที่นั่งเด็กในรถยนต์

- ... quiet room I can use?

  hɔ̂ɔng ngiiap-ngiiap tîi chǎn/pǒm sǎa-mâat chái dâi

  ห้องเงียบๆ ที่ ฉัน/ผม สามารถใช้ได้

Do you have children?

kun mii lûuk mǎi

คุณมีลูกไหม

I'm single.

chǎn/pǒm sòot

ฉัน/ผม โสด

The Kids Are Alright

I'm married.   chăn/pǒm dtèɛng-ngaan lέɛo
ฉัน/ผม แต่งงานแล้ว

And for the picky eaters in the family -

Is there a... nearby?   tɛ̀ɛo níi mii...mǎi
แถวนี้มี...ไหม

- ...McDonald's...   mɛ̂ɛk-doo-nan
  แมคโดนัลด์

- ...Burger King...   bəə-gə̂ə-king
  เบอร์เกอร์คิง

- ...KFC...   kee-èep-sii
  เคเอฟซี

- ...Ice cream parlour...   ráan ai-sà-griim
  ร้านไอศกรีม

- ... Starbucks...   sà-dtaa-bàk
  สตาร์บัคส์

20. Let's Go to the Movies [4]

What movies are playing?
 nǎng rûuang à-rai gam-lang kâo-roong yùu
 หนังเรื่องอะไรกำลังเข้าโรงอยู่

I'd like two tickets to see.... please.
 chǎn/pǒm yàak dâi dtǔua sǒɔng bai pûua duu rûuang...
 ฉัน/ผม อยากได้ตั๋วสองใบเพื่อดูเรื่อง...

Is.... sold out?
 ...kǎai mòt lɛ́ɛo rə̌ə
 ...ขายหมดแล้วเหรอ

When is the next show time?
 rɔ̂ɔp dtɔ̀ɔ-bpai gìi moong
 รอบต่อไป กี่โมง

What time does the movie start?
 nǎng rə̂əm chǎai gìi moong
 หนังเริ่มฉาย กี่โมง

I'd like the ... show please.
 chǎn/pǒm yàak dâi rɔ̂ɔp...
 ฉัน/ผม อยากได้รอบ...

- ...3 o'clock...
 bàai sǎam moong
 บ่ายสามโมง

- ...4 o'clock...
 sìi moong yen
 สี่โมงเย็น

- ...5 o'clock...
 hâa moong yen
 ห้าโมงเย็น

---

[4] Remember to have a sweater handy, cinemas are notoriously well air-conditioned

Let's Go to the Movies

- …6 o'clock…
  hòk moong yen
  หกโมงเย็น

How much are... tickets?
kâa dtŭua săm-ráp…tâo-rai
ค่าตั๋วสำหรับ…เท่าไร

- …regular…
  kon tûua-bpai
  คนทั่วไป

- …student…
  nák-riian
  นักเรียน

I'd like a seat near the front.
chăn/pŏm yàak dâi tîi-nâng dâan nâa
ฉัน/ผม อยากได้ที่นั่งด้านหน้า

I'd like a seat near the back.
chăn/pŏm yàak dâi tîi-nâng dâan lăng
ฉัน/ผม อยากได้ที่นั่งด้านหลัง

Is the movie in English or Thai?
năng bpen paa-săa ang-grìt rŭɯ tai
หนังเป็นภาษาอังกฤษหรือไทย

Are there English subtitles?
mii kam-bplɛɛ paa-săa ang-grìt măi
มีคำแปลภาษาอังกฤษไหม

Please stand.
gà-rú-naa yɯɯn
กรุณายืน

This is the King's anthem.
nîi kɯɯ pleeng săn-sŏən prá-baa-rá-mii
นี่คือเพลงสรรเสริญพระบารมี

21. Where's the Party

Would you like to join me for a drink?	kun yàak dùɯm dûuai-gan sàk-gɛ̂ɛo mǎi

คุณอยากดื่มด้วยกันสักแก้วไหม

Where is a good place for...   tîi dii-dii sǎm-ràp...yùu tîi-nǎi

ที่ดีๆ สำหรับ...อยู่ที่ไหน

- ...dancing?   dtêen-ram

  เต้นรำ

- ...jazz?   don-dtrii-jɛ́ɛt

  ดนตรีแจ๊ส

- ...local music?   don-dtrii púɯn-bâan

  ดนตรีพื้นบ้าน

- ...cheap drinks?   krûɯang-dùɯm raa-kaa mâi pɛɛng

  เครื่องดื่มราคาไม่แพง

- ...a quiet drink?   nâng dùɯm ngiiap-ngiiap

  นั่งดื่มเงียบๆ

- ...karaoke?   rɔ́ɔng kaa-raa-oo-gè

  ร้องคาราโอเกะ

Let's go somewhere else.   bpai tîi-ùɯn gan tè

ไปที่อื่นกันเถอะ

Is there a cover charge?   mii kâa bɔɔ-rí-gaan mǎi

มีค่าบริการไหม

What time do you close?   kun bpìt gìi moong

คุณปิดกี่โมง

Where's the Party?

I'd like to buy a drink for that man.	chăn/pŏm yàak súu krûuang-dùum hâi pûu-chaai kon nán

ฉัน/ผม อยากซื้อเครื่องดื่มให้ผู้ชายคนนั้น

I'd like to buy a drink for that woman.	chăn/pŏm yàak súu krûuang-dùum hâi pûu-yĭng kon nán

ฉัน/ผม อยากซื้อเครื่องดื่มให้ผู้หญิงคนนั้น

I missed you so much.	chăn/pŏm kít-tŭng kun mâak

ฉัน/ผม คิดถึงคุณมาก

I love you.	chăn/pŏm rák kun

ฉัน/ผม รักคุณ

I love you a lot.	chăn/pŏm rák kun mâak

ฉัน/ผม รักคุณมาก

22. Some Toilet Talk

In the Restrooms

Please do not flush... down the toilet.	gà-rú-naa yàa tíng...long nai tŏo sûuam

กรุณาอย่าทิ้ง...ลงในโถส้วม

- ...tampons / sanitary napkins... pâa a-naa-mai

  ผ้าอนามัย

- ... toilet paper... grà-dàat cham-rá

  กระดาษชำระ

- ... trash... kà-yà

  ขยะ

- ... condoms... tŭng-yaang à-naa-mai

  ถุงยางอนามัย

- ... stockings (* this is in the ladies toilets at Suvarnabumi airport)...

    tŭng-nɔ̂ɔng

    ถุงน่อง

Please use the bin provided.

gà-rú-naa tíng long tăng kà-yà

กรุณาทิ้งลงถังขยะ

Is there...

mii...măi

มี...ไหม

- ... toilet paper?

    grà-dàat cham-rá

    กระดาษชำระ

- ... soap?

    sà-bùu

    สบู่

- ... a hand towel?

    pâa-chét-muu

    ผ้าเช็ดมือ

- ... western toilet?

    chák-krôok

    ชักโครก

- ... squat toilet?

    sûuam-sum

    ส้วมซึม

23. Are you Traveling Alone?

Are you travelling alone?   kun dəən-tang kon-diiao châi măi
คุณเดินทางคนเดียวใช่ไหม

No, I'm traveling with my...   mâi *[pause]* chăn/pŏm dəən-taang gàp...
ไม่ ฉัน/ผม เดินทางกับ...

- ...friend.   pûuan
  เพื่อน

- ...friends.   pûuan-pûuan
  เพื่อนๆ

- ...wife.   pan-rá-yaa
  ภรรยา

- ...husband.   săa-mii
  สามี

- ...mother.   mɛ̂ɛ
  แม่

- ...father.   pɔ̂ɔ
  พ่อ

- ...parents.   pɔ̂ɔ lɛ́ɛ mɛ̂ɛ
  พ่อและแม่

- ...older sister.   pîi-săao
  พี่สาว

- ...younger sister.   nɔ́ɔng-săao
  น้องสาว

The Perfect Thai Phrasebook

- ...older brother.   pîi-chaai
  พี่ชาย

- ...younger brother.   nɔ́ɔng-chaai
  น้องชาย

- ...girlfriend / boyfriend.   fɛɛn
  แฟน

Where do you work?   kun tam-ngaan tîi-nǎi
คุณทำงานที่ไหน

What work do you do?   kun tam-ngaan à-rai
คุณทำงานอะไร

I am...   chǎn/pǒm bpen...
ฉัน/ผม เป็น...

- ...a teacher.   kruu
  ครู

- ...a student.   nák-riian
  นักเรียน

- ...a business man/woman.   nák-tú-rá-gìt
  นักธุรกิจ

- ... an engineer.   wít-sà-wá-gɔɔn
  วิศวกร

I am unemployed.   chǎn/pǒm dtòk ngaan
ฉัน/ผม ตกงาน

I am retired.   chǎn/pǒm gà-sǐian lɛ́ɛo
ฉัน/ผม เกษียณแล้ว

I am self-employed.   chǎn/pǒm tam tú-rá-gìt sùuan-dtuua
ฉัน/ผม ทำธุรกิจส่วนตัว

Are Your Travelling Alone?

What do you like to do in...?	kun chɔ̂ɔp tam à-rai tîi...
	คุณชอบทำอะไรที่...
The weather today is...	wan-níi aa-gàat...
	วันนี้อากาศ...
• ...lovely.	dii
	ดี
• ... terrible.	mâi dii
	ไม่ดี
• ... hot.	rɔ́ɔn
	ร้อน
• ... rainy.	mǔuan fǒn jà dtok
	เหมือนฝนจะตก
Can you take a photo of us?	kun chûuai tàai-rûup hâi pûuak-rao nɔ̀ɔi dâi mǎi
	คุณช่วยถ่ายรูปให้พวกเราหน่อยได้ไหม
Press this button.	gòt bpùm níi
	กดปุ่มนี้
Can I take a photo of you?	chǎn/pǒm kɔ̌ɔ tàai-rûup kun dâi mǎi
	ฉัน/ผม ขอถ่ายรูปคุณได้ไหม
You have a very lovely smile.	kun yím sǔuai mâak
	คุณยิ้มสวยมาก

24. Keeping Busy (Things to See and Do)

I'm looking for (a)... chăn/pŏm gam-lang moong hăa...
ฉัน/ผม กำลังมองหา...

- ...massage place. ráan nûuat
  ร้านนวด

- ... night market. dtà-làat glaang-kɯɯn
  ตลาดกลางคืน

- ... museum. pí-pít-tá-pan
  พิพิธภัณฑ์

- ... quiet beach. hàat ngîiap-ngîiap
  หาดเงียบๆ

- ... party beach. hàat tîi mii ngaan-líiang
  หาดที่มีงานเลี้ยง

- ... waterfall. nám-dtòk
  น้ำตก

- ... Muay Thai (Thai kickboxing) match. gaan kɛ̀ɛng-kăn muuai-tai
  การแข่งขันมวยไทย

- ... temple. wát
  วัด

25. Life on the Wild Side

I want to go to a...	chǎn/pǒm dtôong-gaan bpai...
	ฉัน/ผม ต้องการไป...
• ...snake farm.	faam nguu
	ฟาร์มงู
• ...elephant show.	tîi sà-dɛɛng cháang
	ที่แสดงช้าง
• ... elephant sanctuary.	kèet sà-ngǔuan pan cháang
	เขตสงวนพันธุ์ช้าง
• ...tiger park.	sǔuan sǔɯa
	สวนเสือ
• ...zoo.	sǔuan sàt
	สวนสัตว์
• ...night safari.	nai saa-faa-rii
	ไนท์ซาฟารี
• ... water buffalo farm.	faam kwaai
	ฟาร์มควาย

26. Learn a Little

I want to take a... class	chǎn/pǒm dtôong-gaan riian...
	ฉัน/ผม ต้องการเรียน...
• ...cooking...	gaan tam aa-hǎan
	การทำอาหาร
• ...massage...	gaan nûuat
	การนวด

- ...meditation...   gaan tam sà-maa-tí
  การทำสมาธิ
- ...Thai language...   paa-săa tai
  ภาษาไทย
- ...scuba diving...   dam-náam lúk
  ดำน้ำลึก
- ...Muay Thai...   muuai-tai
  มวยไทย

27. Important Personages

Use these words with caution and respect

- King   nai-lŭuang
  ในหลวง
- Queen   prá-raa-chí-nii
  พระราชินี
- Royal Family   prá-bà-rom-má-wong-săa-nú-wong
  พระบรมวงศานุวงศ์
- Buddha   prá-pút-tá-jâo
  พระพุทธเจ้า
- Monk   prá-sŏng
  พระสงฆ์
- Novice Monks   neen
  เณร
- Shrine   săan-jâo
  ศาลเจ้า

Appendix

Appendix A. Verbs

Ask	tăam (ถาม)
Bite	gàt (กัด)
Brush	bprɛɛg (แปรง)
Climb	bpiin (ปีน)
Come	maa (มา)
Cook	tam aa-hăan (ทำอาหาร)
Cry	rɔ́ɔng-hâi (ร้องไห้)
Cut	dtàt (ตัด)
Dance	dtêen-ram (เต้นรำ)
Do	tam (ทำ)
Drink	dùɯm (ดื่ม)
Drive	kàp (ขับ)
Eat	gin (กิน)
Find	jəə (เจอ)
Forget	lɯɯm (ลืม)
Go	bpai (ไป)
Have	mii (มี)
Hear	dâi-yin (ได้ยิน)
Help	chûai (ช่วย)
Jump	grà-dòot (กระโดด)
Know (something)	rúu (รู้)
Know (someone)	rúu-jàk (รู้จัก)
Like	chɔ̂ɔp (ชอบ)
Listen	fang (ฟัง)
Look	duu (ดู)
Look for	mɔɔng-hăa (มองหา)

Appendices

Love	rák (รัก)
Meet	póp (พบ)
Need	jam-bpen-dtɔ̂ɔng (จำเป็นต้อง)
Play	lêen (เล่น)
Pull	dɯng (ดึง)
Push	plàk (ผลัก)
Put (down)	waang (วาง)
Read	àan (อ่าน)
Remember	jam (จำ)
Ride	kìi (ขี่)
Run	wîng (วิ่ง)
See	hĕn (เห็น)
Sing	rɔ́ɔng-pleeng (ร้องเพลง)
Sit	nâng (นั่ง)
Sleep	nɔɔn (นอน)
Stand	yɯɯn (ยืน)
Study	riian (เรียน)
Swim	wâai (ว่าย)
Teach	sɔ̌ɔn (สอน)
Think	kít (คิด)
Understand	kâo-jai (เข้าใจ)
Use	chái (ใช้)
Walk	dəən (เดิน)
Want	dtɔ̂ɔng-gaan (ต้องการ)
Watch	fâo-duu (เฝ้าดู)
Write	kĭian (เขียน)

Appendix B. Adjectives

Big	yài (ใหญ่)
Little	nít-nɔ̀ɔi (นิดหน่อย)
Fast	réo (เร็ว)
Slow	cháa (ช้า)
Happy	mii kwaam sùk (มีความสุข)
Sad	sâo (เศร้า)
Long	yaao (ยาว)
Short	dtîia (เตี้ย)
Loud	dang (ดัง)
Quiet	ngîiap (เงียบ)
Tall	sǔung (สูง)
Small	lék (เล็ก)
Angry	gròot (โกรธ)
Difficult, hard	yâak (ยาก)
Warm (friendly)	òp-ùn (อบอุ่น)
Friendly	bpen-mít (เป็นมิตร)
Hostile	mâi bpen-mít (ไม่เป็นมิตร)
Hard, heavy	nàk (หนัก)
Easy	ngâai (ง่าย)
Light (weight)	bao (เบา)
Dark	mʉʉt (มืด)
Light (bright)	sà-wàang (สว่าง)
Good	dii (ดี)
Bad	leeo (เลว)
Beautiful	sǔuai (สวย)
Ugly	nâa-glìat (น่าเกลียด)

Appendices

Hungry .... hǐo (หิว)
Full (up - with food) .... ìm (อิ่ม)
Strong .... kěng-rɛɛng (แข็งแรง)
Weak .... ɔ̀ɔn-ɛɛ (อ่อนแอ)
Old .... gào (เก่า)
Young (adolescent) .... nùm (male), sǎao (female) (หนุ่ม, สาว)
Rich .... ruuai (รวย)
Poor .... jon (จน)
Expensive .... pɛɛng (แพง)
Cheap .... tùuk (ถูก)

Appendix C. Food and Cooking

Food and cooking are [almost] a national pastime in Thailand. Going out, meeting with friends, after work, all these events are based around food. The folllowing sections help you with some food and cooking terms.

Appendix C.1. Cooking Terms

Boil .... dtôm (ต้ม)
Steam .... nûng (นึ่ง)
.... (you may also hear it being called dtǔn (ตุ๋น))
Deep fried .... tɔ̂ɔt (ทอด)
Toast .... bpîng (ปิ้ง)
Bake .... òp (อบ)
Barbeque, grill, roast .... yâang (ย่าง)
Fry .... pàt (ผัด)

Appendix C.2. Commenting

Delicious .... à-ròoi (อร่อย)

Not delicious .... mâi à-ròoi (ไม่ อร่อย)

Very delicious .... à-ròoi mâak (อร่อยมาก)

Spicy .... pèt (เผ็ด)

Not spicy .... mâi pèt (ไม่เผ็ด)

Very Spicy .... pèt mâak (เผ็ดมาก)

Sweet .... wăan (หวาน)

Sour .... bprîiao (เปรี้ยว)

Salty .... kem (เค็ม)

Bitter .... kŏm (ขม)

Appendix C.3. Food

Rice .... kâao (ข้าว)

.... or you may see ข้าวสวย (kâao sŭuai - cooked rice)

Sticky rice .... kâao nĭiao (ข้าวเหนียว)

Chicken .... gài (ไก่)

Pork .... mŭu (หมู)

Beef .... núua (เนื้อ)

Fish .... bplaa (ปลา)

Chilli .... prík (พริก)

Mushroom .... hèt (เห็ด)

Onion .... hŏom-hŭa-yài (หอมหัวใหญ่)

Appendices

Appendix C.4. Dishes

A selection of some of our favourite Thai dishes:

Chicken with chillies	gài pàt prík yùak (ไก่ผัดพริกหยวก)
Chicken with basil and chillies	gà-prao gài (กะเพราไก่)
Noodles	gŭuai-dtĭiao (ก๋วยเตี๋ยว)
Green sweet chicken curry	gɛɛng kĭiao wăan gài (แกงเขียวหวานไก่)
Thai vermicelli	kà-nŏm jiin (ขนมจีน)
Rice soup	kâao dtôm (ข้าวต้ม)
Spicy soup with shrimp	dtôm yam gûng (ต้มยำกุ้ง)
Spicy soup with chicken	dtôm yam gài (ต้มยำไก่)
Noodles Thai style	pàd tai (ผัดไทย)
Omelette	kài jiiao (ไข่เจียว)
Papaya salad	sôm-dtam (ส้มตำ)
Minced pork salad	lâap (ลาบ)

Appendix C.5. Drinks

Water	nám (น้ำ)
Orange	sôm (ส้ม)
Orange juice	nám sôm (น้ำส้ม)
Grapefruit	sôm-oo (ส้มโอ)
Grapefruit juice	nám sôm-oo (น้ำส้มโอ)
Pineapple	sàp-bpà-rót (สับปะรด)
Coffee	gaa-fɛɛ (กาแฟ)
Tea	chaa (ชา)
Coke	kóok (โค้ก)
Ice	náam kɛ́ng (น้ำแข็ง)

Beer	biia (เบียร์)
Wine	wai (ไวน์)

Appendix C.6. Culinary Items

Plate / dish	jaan (จาน)
Cup	tûuai (ถ้วย)
Bowl	chaam (ชาม)
Glass	gɛ̂ɛo (แก้ว)
Knife	mîit (มีด)
Fork	sɔ̂ɔm (ส้อม)
Spoon	chɔ́ɔn (ช้อน)

Index

7/11, 45
Accident, *64*
Add, 51
Adolescent, 85
Aeroplane ticket, 40
Age, 23, *67*
Air conditioner, 36, 39
Airport, 35, 40
Aisle seat, 44
Alcohol, 56
Allergic, 53
America, 20
Angry, 84
Antique, *59*
Arrival card, 32
Arrive, 41
Ask, *82*
Aspirin, *66*
ATM, *60*
Authentic, *59*
Baby bottles, *68*
Baby formula, *68*
Baby wipes, *68*
Back, *71*
Bad, 84
Bag, *60, 63*
Bake, 85
Band-aids, *66*
Bank, 49, *60*
Bar, 50
Barbeque, 85
Bathroom, 26, 39
Bathtub, 36
Beach, 34, 49, *78*
Beautiful, 84
Bedroom, 39
Beef, 52, 86
Beer, 56, 88
Behind, 45
Bicycle, 48
Big, 84
Bigger size, *58*
Bin, *74*
Bite, *82*
Bitter, 86
Blister, *66*
Blood, 52
Boil, 85
Bottle, 55
Bottled water, 36
Boyfriend, *76*
Breakfast, 37
Brush, 82
BTS Station, 51
Buddha, *80*
Burger King, *69*
Bus, 46
Bus station, 35, 40
Bus ticket, 40
Business card, *60*
Business traveller, 30
Businessman, 23, *76*
Button, *77*
Buy, 40, *67*
Buy a drink, *73*
Campsite, 31
Canada, 20
Cannot, 19
Car, 46, 48
Car seat, *68*
Certificate of authenticity, *59*
Cheap, 85
Cheap drinks, *72*
Check-in, 37
Check-out, 37
Cheerio, 22
Chemist, *65*
Chicken, 52, 86
Chicken with basil and chillies, 87
Chicken with chillies, 87
Children, *68*
Chilli, 86
Chinese restaurant, 50
Chocolate, 55
Church, 50
Cinema tickets, *71*
City, 34
Clean, 38
Climb, *82*
Close, *60, 72*
Coffee, 55, 87
Coke, 87
Cold, *66*
Cold drink, 54
Colour, *58*
Come, 27, 82
Come from, 32
Condensed milk, *57*
Condoms, *67, 73*
Congratulations, 25
Consulate, *64*
Cook, 82
Cooking, *79*
Cotton, *59*
Country, 20, 23, 34
Cover charge, *72*
Credit card, 38
Crib, *68*
Cry, 82
Cup, 55, 88
Currency exchange, *60*
Cut, 82
Dance, 82
Dancing, *72*
Dark, 84
Date of Birth, 34
Daughter, *67*
Day, 21
Deep fried, 85
Delicious, 25, 86
Dentist, *63*

The Perfect Thai Phrasebook

Deodorant, *67*
Depart, 41
Departure card, 32
Diapers, *68*
Diarrhoea, *66*
Difficult, 19, 84
Discount, *58*
Dish, 88
Do, 24, 82
Doctor, *63*
Dollars, *61*
Don't add, 52
Don't know, 28
Drain, 39
Drink, *72*, 82
Drive, 82
Drug store, 49, *65*
Durian, 37
Earlier, 43
Earthquake, *65*
Easy, 19, 84
Eat, 82
Eight, 30
Elephant sanctuary, *79*
Elephant show, *79*
Embassy, *64*
Engineer, *76*
English, 19
English menu, 52
Euros, *61*
Evening, 29
Exchange rate, *61*
Excuse me, 24, 55
Expensive, *58*, 85
Fan, 36, 39
Fast, 84
Father, *75*
Female, 13
Feminine hygiene products, *67*
Ferry terminal, 40
Ferry ticket, 40
Find, 46, 82
First name, 33
Fish, 86
Five, 30

Flood, *65*
Forget, 82
Fork, 88
Four, 30
Fridge, 36
Fried egg, 52
Friend, *75*
Friendly, 84
Front, 45, *71*
Fry, 85
Full (up - with food), 85
Garden view, 38
Gas station, 49
Girlfriend, *76*
Glass, 55, 88
Go, 82
Go straight, 44
Going, 21
Good, 84
Good luck, 25
Goodnight, 22, 25
Grapefruit, 87
Grapefruit juice, 87
Green sweet chicken curry, 87
grill, 85
Guesthouse, 31
Hand towel, *74*
Happy, 84
Happy birthday, 25
Happy New Year, 25
Hard (heavy), 84
Hard (not easy), 84
Have, 82
He / She, 29
Headache, *65*
Hear, 82
Heavy, 84
Hello, 18
Help, 26, 82
Here, 29
Him / Her, 29
Hostel, 31
Hostile, 84
Hot, 21, *77*

Hot drink, 54
Hot water (washing), 36
Hotel, 31, 34, 45, 49
How, 26
How much, 36, 46
Hungry, 21, 85
Hurry up, *58*
Husband, *75*
I'm sorry (apology), 24
I'm sorry (upset), 24
Ice, *57*, 87
Ice cream parlour, *69*
Immigration Office, 32
Imodium, *66*
Indian restaurant, 50
Jazz, *72*
Jump, 82
Karaoke, *72*
KFC, *69*
Kind, 24
King, *80*
Knife, 88
Know (someone), 82
Know (something), 82
Later, 44
Lawyer, *65*
Learn, 23
Left, 45
Light (bright), 84
Light (weight), 84
Like, 23, 82
Listen, 82
Little, 84
Live, 20
Local music, *72*
Long, 84
Look, 26, *58*, 82
Look for, 82
Lost, 26

Index

Loud, 84
Love, 73, 83
Lovely, 77
Luggage, 38, 44
mâi bpen rai, 6
Malaysian restaurant, 50
Male, 13
Market, 34, 49
Married, 69
Massage, 78, 79
McDonald's, 69
Me, 29
Meditation, 80
Meet, 83
Mexican restaurant, 50
Milk, 57
Minced pork salad, 87
Month, 21
Morning, 29
Mosque, 50
Mother, 75
Motorcycle, 46, 48
Movie, 70
Movie tickets, 71
MRT Station (Bangkok Underground), 51
Muay Thai match, 78
Museum, 50, 78
Mushroom, 86
Name, 18
Nationality, 34
Natural Disasters, 65
Nearest, 49
Need, 83
New Zealand, 64
Night, 29
Night market, 78
Night safari, 79
Night-club, 35
Nine, 30
No problem, 27

Non-smoking, 37
Noodles, 53, 87
Noodles Thai style, 87
Not delicious, 86
Not expensive, 58
Not spicy, 86
Novice Monks, 80
Now, 29
Nuts, 53
Ocean view, 39
O'clock, 70
Old, 23, 85
Older brother, 76
Older sister, 75
Omelette, 87
One, 30
One-way (single) ticket, 42
Onion, 86
Open, 60
Orange, 87
Orange juice, 87
Ovaltine, 55
Papaya salad, 87
Parents, 75
Park, 48
Party beach, 78
Passport, 30, 63
Petrol station, 49
Pets, 37
Pharmacy, 26, 49, 65
Phone, 64
Photo, 77
Photocopy, 33
Photos, 33
Pineapple, 87
Place of Birth, 34
Plane ticket, 40
Plate, 88
Play, 83
Please, 19
Police, 63
Police station, 49
Poor, 85
Pork, 52, 86

Post office, 50
Pounds, 61
Price, 57
Problem, 39
Province, 34
Pull, 83
Push, 83
Put (down), 83
Queen, 80
Quiet, 84
Quiet beach, 78
Quiet drink, 72
Quiet room, 68
Rainy, 77
Rash, 66
Read, 83
Really, 58
Red wine, 56
Remember, 83
Rent, 48
Reservation, 37
Restaurant, 35, 49
Restaurant car, 43
Retired, 76
Rice, 53, 86
Rice soup, 87
Rich, 85
Ride, 83
Right, 45
roast, 85
Room, 35, 39
Room key, 63
Room service, 38
Round-trip (return) ticket, 42
Royal Family, 80
Run, 83
Sad, 84
Safe, 36
Salt, 56
Salty, 86
Sanitary napkins, 73
Scuba diving, 80
Seafood, 53
Seat (travel), 42
See, 83

Self-employed, *76*
Sell, *57*
Service charge, 53
Seven, 30
Shellfish, 53
Ship overseas, *59*
Short, 84
Shower, 36
Shower (electric shower), 39
Shrine, *80*
Shuttle bus, 35
Silk, *59*
Sing, 83
Single (unmarried), *68*
Sink, 39
Sit, 83
Six, 30
Sleep, 83
Sleeping car, 42
Slow, 84
Slow taxi, 46
Small, 84
Smaller size, *58*
Smile, *77*
Smoke, 55
Smoking, 37
Smoothie, 56
Snake farm, *79*
Soap, *74*
Sold out, *70*
Sour, 86
South African, *65*
Speak, 19
Speak Thai, 19
Spicy, 86
Spicy food, 51
Spicy soup with chicken, 87
Spicy soup with shrimp, 87
Spoon, 88
Squat toilet, *74*
Stand, 83
Starbucks, *69*
Station, 45

Station - bus station, 35
Station - train station, 35
Steam, 85
Sticking plasters, *66*
Sticky rice, 86
Stockings, *74*
Stomach ache, *66*
Stop, 45
Stroller, *68*
Strong, 85
Student, 30, *76*
Study, 83
Subtitles, *71*
Sugar, *57*
Sunburn, *66*
Sunscreen, *66*, *68*
Supermarket, 50
Surname, 33
Sweet, 86
Sweet dreams, 25
Swim, 83
Syrup, *57*
Tall, 84
Tampons, *73*
Taxi, 46
  – Slow taxi, 46
Tea, 55, 87
Teach, 83
Teacher, *76*
Temple, 35, 50, *78*
Ten, 30
Terrible/bad, *77*
Thai kickboxing match, *78*
Thai vermicelli, 87
Thank you, 14
Thank you very much, 14, 15
That, 29
The King's anthem, *71*
There, 29
They / Them, 29
Think, 83

Thirsty, 21
This, 29
Three, 30
Ticket, 40
Ticket window, 41
Tickets, *63*
Tiger balm, *66*
Tiger park, *79*
Time, 29, *70*
Tired, 21
Toast, 85
Today, 29
Toilet, 39
Toilet paper, *73*
Tomorrow, 29, 47, *60*
Toothpaste, *67*
Tour, 38
Tourist, 30
Tourist police, *64*
Traffic lights, 45
Train station, 35, 40
Train ticket, 40
Translator, 23, *65*
Trash, *73*
Travel agent, 41
Traveler's cheques, *61*
Truck, 46
Tsunami, *65*
Tuk-tuk, 46
Turkish restaurant, 50
TV, 36, 39
Two, 30
Tylenol, *66*
Ugly, 84
Understand, 32, 83
Unemployed, *76*
Use, 83
Vegetables, 52
Vegetarian, 51
Very delicious, 86
Very Spicy, 86
Visa, 31
Wait, 47
Wake up, 38

Index

Walk, 83
Wallet, *63*
Want, 83
Warm (friendly), 84
Watch, 83
Water, 55, 87
Water buffalo farm, *79*
Waterfall, *78*
We / Us, 29
Weak, 85
Weather, *77*
Week, 21
Welcome, 18
Western food, 52
Western toilet, *74*
What?, 25
Wheat (gluten), 53
When?, 26
Where?, 26
Whiskey, 56
White wine, 56
Who?, 25
Why?, 26
wife, *75*
Wi-Fi, 37
Window, 39
Window seat, 44
Wine, 88
Work, 23, *76*
Write, 27, 83
Yen, *61*
Yesterday, 29
You, 29
Young (adolescent), 85
Younger brother, *76*
Younger sister, *75*
Zoo, *79*

Bibliography

Crowley, R., & Mondi, D. W. (2011). *Learnng Thai, Your Great Adventure.* Cardiff: R Crowley.

Slayden, G. (2010, November 5th). *History of Thai Language*. Retrieved May 26th, 2012, from Thai-Language.com: http://www.thai-language.com/ref/Overview

Thai language. (2012, May 21). Retrieved May 26, 2012, from Wikipedia: http://en.wikipedia.org/wiki/Thai_language

A Note From the Authors

Thanks for buying and reading through *The Perfect Thai Phrasebook*, the third book in our series. When we were writing *Learning Thai, Your Great Adventure,* our first book, we already had the idea for *Memory Aids to Your Great Adventure* AND we knew we wanted more phrases and day-to-day information to add to *LTYGA;* but, given the time aspect, the ever-increasing page count, that it was our first foray into publishing (self or otherwise), and other apsects (such as work and study), we felt that we need a bit of time before creating this book.

In the British Army, on vacation, and as part of his work sailing yachts, Russ has travelled to over 100 countries and has come across many types of phrasebook, some useful, others not. It's great having a book with every conceivable phrase in it; but, one of the big problems with any kind of communication is though you can point at, or ask the question yourself, you are then lost when the reply comes back. At that point, hundreds of pages of size 7 font isn't much use to you.

You need something simple, something which is easy to follow, and is something that is actually used. So, we sat down and discussed what would fill this particular need and, as we've mentioned before, to also create something which then wouldn't be redundant if you ever decided to take your Thai language studies further.

This resulting phrasebook is designed so that you can use it at the beginner stage; but, and equally importantly, as we've deliberately made the Thai script larger – this current sentence is Arial Unicode size 9, but Thai font at the same size is สวัสดีครับ – it can also be used all the way through your Thai language studies to the point where you have successfully reached the goal of your *Quest* – and that is just perfect!

Our Other Products

The Learn Thai Alphabet application

The *Learn Thai Alphabet application* lets you learn the alphabet interactively with quizzes, games, test reviews, native Thai speakers, drag-and-drop games, and much more.

If you have enjoyed this book and would like to help us, if you could leave an honest review of this book on the page or the website where you got it from, you'd be helping us out a great deal – thank you.

The above products are available at http://www.learnthaialphabet.com

Printed in Great Britain
by Amazon